ECHOES OF THE ARCANE

A COLLECTION OF SHORT FICTION
CODY D. CAMPBELL

WRAITHWOOD PRESS

Book Cover designed by Cody D. Campbell

Wolf and Moon by Ruslan Bond via Canva

Decorative Line Border by sumit via Canva

Wraithwood Press

wraithwoodpress.com

Library of Congress Control Number: 2024934035

First edition: April 2024

Paperback ISBN: 979-8-9889175-0-2

Digital ISBN: 979-8-9889175-1-9

For everyone who ever felt like they weren't enough.

FOREWORD

Dear readers,

Let me start by thanking you for picking up *Echoes of the Arcane*. I first sat down to write some of these stories over a decade before they found their way into your hands. I'm honored beyond words that you've decided to read them. I feel that it is my duty, however, to warn you that many of the stories in these pages are quite heavy. They deal with themes of loss, abandonment, bitterness, and often hopelessness. They use teleportation devices and folktales of ancient frogmen as a lens, but many of them are ultimately about the times when things simply fall apart. Times when all we can do is carry on despite overwhelming despair. I use the word 'bittersweet' to describe these stories. My wife uses the word 'depressing.' I hope that you'll read them with an open mind and, more importantly, an open heart. Some of them will hurt, but I have found that pain is often where we discover our greatest strengths.

For me, that is best encapsulated by *Last of the Legion*, which is both the oldest and the longest story in this collection. I wrote the first draft in 2013, with the ambitious intent for it to feel like an ancient epic akin to *The Iliad*. Instead, I ended up with a generic piece of historical fiction that was riddled with tedious exposition. I came back to it many times over the years, trying again and again to turn it into something worthwhile, and each time feeling more beaten down when I failed.

It was my boulder and fixing it was my hill. My failures made me feel hollow, like an echo of the person I thought I was. I felt like not being able to turn this story into something worthwhile meant that I wasn't the writer I thought I was, and that maybe I never would be.

I did fix it in the end, I think. I at least got to a point where I'm comfortable sharing it with you all. I don't know if I'll ever look back on the anguish and tears that went into making it and think that it was worth the suffering that went into its creation, but now, at last, I can finally put the boulder down.

I think everyone feels that way sometimes. Like, maybe we're not the person we think we are. Maybe we're just this shell, trying to convince the world we're actually whole, even though we secretly know there's nothing inside. I don't think it's true though.

We are more than echoes.

-Cody

CONTENTS

LITTLE BUGS

I finally walked in the woods again today. They were closed to the public for fifteen years, but now I was free to pick through the familiar trails. The paths were quiet this morning, except for the soft buzzing of tiny metal bugs. I supposed they must have been empty during the quarantine too, back when you couldn't breathe without choking on poison. The forest sat right on the border of my grandma's property. It was less than two miles from the Yuba River. My tire swing was just beyond its edge. I remember crying when they told me I couldn't use it anymore. It was past the government line.

The men who came to tell us about the quarantine were wearing green overalls. They reminded me of the ones my grandpa used to wear to his plumbing job before he retired. They told us they were from the government. We'd just gotten home from the county fair and my face was still covered in orange and black makeup where the vendor had painted it to look like a tiger's. Grandma made them iced tea, and they came inside to explain why we couldn't go into the woods anymore. They showed us the barriers they were going to set up to let us know how far into the woods was considered safe. Then they showed us the bugs.

They were shiny little things, like a dime that had gone through the wash in your pocket. They twitched around the men's fingers like normal insects, but they weren't really bugs at all. They were tiny robots that scientists had made to eat the poison and turn it into fertilizer for the plants. Grandma laughed when she saw them and clapped her hands. She thought they were funny. Grandpa frowned, his bushy gray eyebrows burrowing down the bridge of his nose.

"Get out of my house," he said to them. "You can put up your fences and play with your bugs all you like, but no one comes into my home and tells me to stay out of these woods."

I wondered if I'd find his body in here. Probably not. Tourists flooded the state park after they finally lifted the quarantine. It was the third in the country to be deemed clean, so people came from all over to walk in the trees and be with nature again. If none of them found him, I don't imagine there was much left to find.

A lot of them kept trying to set up camp in my grandma's yard when they were here. I had to chase a few off with Grandpa's old rifle. I never shot it. I didn't even know how. But the sight of a grown woman running through the grass, slinging a rifle and wearing nothing but a bathrobe was enough to send most of them skittering away.

Now the woods were quiet again, the way I remembered them. The ground was crunchy. The old paths were overgrown, and the new ones were still rough around the edges.

I wasn't sure exactly where I was going. I had a vague sense that this was the way he'd taken me when I was little. I remembered holding his hand. It was calloused from working with tools and stained in places from the layers of grease that wouldn't wash away. He had scars that were always fading, but always there. I traced their lines with my thumb. When I got tired, he'd lift me on his shoulders and start to hum. Sometimes he'd pick up the rhythm of something I thought I knew. It would be like an itch on the back of my brain. I'd try to remember which of his records the song had come from, but then he'd change mid-song and start humming something else. After a while, I'd give up on trying to remember and ask him what song it was.

"Sorry," he'd say. "Didn't realize I was doing it."

Thinking about him, I started humming to myself. The slope of the forest curved downward. There was a sharp flavor to the air now. It rode on the breeze, cool and metallic, letting you know there's water nearby. The little bugs were swirling around in the rocks and trees, their metal legs clicking like chimes against a windowpane. I didn't know how to feel about them. They didn't seem to belong here, but then, they were the only reason I could return.

I heard the tinkling song of moving water as the overgrown weeds gave way to smooth river stones under my feet. I pushed aside a thick patch of prickly bushes and saw the glimmering, clear face of the Yuba. The water was high, but the current was moving slowly enough that it would be reasonably safe for a strong swimmer. It was the last place he took me before they sealed it off.

He wanted to take me again after the government men came, but I wouldn't go. He tried to pull me out the door with him. I cried and hid behind my grandma.

"I don't want to," I said. "It's poison. The whole thing is poison. We'll die."

"It's not poison. We'll be fine."

"Leave her be, Charles," my grandma said, putting a hand on her husband's chest. "If you won't listen to me, or those men, or the news on TV, then there's nothing I can do to stop you from being a fool, but you leave Joni out of it."

"It's not poison!" he shouted, but I could see that he didn't really believe it. His hands were clenched and shaking at his sides. His jaw was locked, but his eyes were pleading. He looked lost, like he didn't know where he was without the woods, like they were the needle on a compass that he navigated the whole world from.

"It's the rest of the world that's poison."

That wasn't the last time I saw him, but it may as well have been. Things were never the same after that. He went missing later that year.

I walked over to where the water was pushing gently against the bank. The silt shined in the afternoon sun as it broke and swelled under the pressure of my boots. I squatted down on my heels, twirling my fingers in the water. It felt slippery. Up close, I could see an oily sheen of soapy pinks and blues hovering over the water's surface.

A bunch of spidery silver bugs came bounding over the water, each little hop sending ripples across its surface. They looked like tiny ballerinas, spinning and leaping across glass. I stuck my hands into the cool river and scooped one of them out when it got close, water and all.

It was calm in my cupped hands, gently spinning around the tiny pool. It had four long, slender legs with wide feet to displace its weight. It didn't have a head, but two long needle-like rods were coming out of its belly. I felt a slight tickling on my palms from where one of the needles ejected the freshly cleaned water. It would probably be six or seven years before the river would be safe to swim in, another ten before it was safe to drink from.

My friend Courtney worked for the EPA. She said that the river bugs aren't as good as the forest ones, that they're constantly rusting and needing to be replaced. She said they're mostly for show, anyway. The river does more to clean itself in a month than the bugs could do in a decade. But then, every little bit helps, right?

I hoped Grandpa made it here—that he spent his last day fishing in the crystal-clear eddies that made his lures dance, even if there were no fish left to catch. I hoped that he would be happy his forest was clean again.

I got up to leave when I noticed something red drifting down the river. Forgetting about its oily surface, I waded out into the middle of the water and snatched it before the current could take it away. It was a plastic cup, the kind people used at parties and barbecues. The water had covered it in its thick, viscous film, but it was still new-looking. One of the tourists must have left it.

A shiny cloud of the little bugs buzzed low over the water as they made their way deeper into the forest, their tiny silicon wings beating angrily against the wind. I could feel their frustration. I tucked the plastic cup in my pocket and sighed, the cold water swirling through my overalls and pulling me down. People never learn.

CLEAN SLATE

Terrance tried to remember what kind of cleaning agents he'd used back on Earth. He'd had a lot of janitorial jobs over the years and each of them seemed to prefer a different variety of chemicals for keeping their facilities clean.

He got his first job as a custodian right out of foster care. Kennedy Middle School had him using army surplus ammonia to clean its floors. It reeked to high heaven and the fumes made him light-headed. That job didn't last long though.

Eight weeks in, some students found the bottle of vodka he kept stashed behind the industrial-grade disinfectant. They didn't really drink it. They tried, but the grain alcohol was too strong so none of them could keep it down. Even so, questions were raised when they got caught and it wasn't long before the little thieves admitted where they found the bottle.

Terrance tried to deny the vodka was his. He insisted that he was a bourbon man and suggested that maybe another student had hidden it there — the lock on the door had been broken for weeks after all. But no one bought it.

One of the parents, a man wearing a shirt that said "Keep Calm and Use the Force" over the image of a goblin-like creature, shouted at him until Terrance felt flecks of wet spit hit his cheek. The principal took him aside after it was over.

"I know why you had it," she whispered as if one of the parents might have had their ear pressed against the door. "Sometimes I feel like I can't get through the day without a stiff drink myself. Dealing with these little shits can be a nightmare, you know?"

Her eyes were crinkled as a grim smirk formed at the edges of her mouth.

"I didn't want to fire you, but it'd be my head on the chopping block next if I didn't. Parents these days are as ruthless as the Reds, am I right?"

She paused again with a sad grin, tilting her head expectantly. He knew what she wanted to hear.

"There was nothing you could do," he said.

She smiled and clapped him on the shoulder. Terrance sighed and asked if he could use the school computers to update his resume before he left.

His next job was at a hotel that used watered-down bleach. They didn't want anything that might clash with the already overwhelming smell of swimming pool chlorine, which in turn had to mask the scent of urine. They also had to be sure that it would be able to kill any foot fungus that barefooted guests might have left on its surface.

He saw some interesting people there. It was close to the boardwalk, which meant that a lot of men who'd usually never be seen this far south of Main Street would share an evening of paid company, soaking in chlorinated water before tumbling into starchy, bleached sheets.

Terrance met his wife, Maria, when he worked there. She wasn't a prostitute but a maid, which was lucky. Terrance wouldn't have been able to afford a prostitute. He saw her in the employee lounge.

It was barely more than a closet located right off the main hallway, but there was a small table and a microwave for them to use. He'd sit in the corner and pretend to read a copy of *The Old Man and the Sea,* while he listened to her and her friend chat in Spanish. He didn't understand a word of it, but he liked the way she made it sound. There was a softness about the vowels. He liked the way she said words like *lavandería, depuración,* and *perro.*

One day, her friend called in sick and Maria sat down at the table. She stared at him until he put down his book.

"That must be good," she said pointing at the dog-eared paperback. "You read it every day. What's it about?"

"An old Cuban man who goes fishing."

"¿Si? What happens next?"

"That's pretty much it. No Soviets."

She laughed and her breath smelled like cinnamon. He liked her smile. It reminded him of ring pops and sticky, grass-stained summer nights. They talked every day after that, gazing at each other over microwave burritos. She said they had good chemistry. He said it was probably because they worked with the same chemicals.

His third job was in a building contracted by the government. They had him use a compound called Zep to clean their floors. The label said non-toxic, but his nose disagreed. It smelled like burnt hair and poison. The liquid was a neon green color that almost glowed in the dark. He spent his nights spreading it across the poorly ventilated labyrinth of hallways under the Nevada desert. Eventually, he got used to it. Most people went home before his shift began, so it was rare for him to see anyone.

He didn't have clearance to know what they made there or how they made it. He had to sign a contract that basically said they'd own his grandchildren if he ever told anyone what he saw there. All Terrance knew was that someone needed to clean the floors. Besides, the snippets of conversation he did manage to overhear between the military men and the company scientists may as well have been Martian for all the sense it made. He never felt comfortable there, but Maria was pregnant with Trina by then and they needed the money.

Still, sometimes he worried he might see something he wasn't supposed to. He pictured himself stumbling into a room where an alien was being cut open by men in yellow hazmat suits. Then he'd wake up in New Mexico with no idea who he was and a suspicious scar on his temple.

He'd been working there for six months when he met Erik Kusme. Terrance saw the 2036 Nobel Science Laureate arrive just as he was leaving at the end of his shift. The CTO was walking, eyes fixed on the device in his palm, when he stepped in front of a silver Magnet Model 2.1 that was barreling down the lane.

Terrance didn't consider himself an especially brave man. He probably would have needed a new pair of underwear at the mere thought of diving in front of a moving car if he'd taken the time to think about it, but his body seemed to move on instinct. He tackled the billionaire out of the magnetic car's path. Four bodyguards had pistols trained on the janitor's head before the two men hit the pavement.

"Put those away you idiots," Kusme hissed at the guards. He pushed his way out from under Terrance and got to his feet, taking a moment to brush the debris from the road off his suit.

Terrance tried to stand up, but he doubled over when he felt the blood rushing to his head. He put his hands on his knees to keep them from shaking.

"I almost died!" the billionaire continued shouting at the guards. "You want to shoot the man who just saved my life? Where were you just now, eh?"

It was odd watching these men hang their heads as the billionaire scolded them. Each of his guards was the size of a young rhinoceros and Kusme barely reached Terrance's shoulder. "A fortune I spend on this incompetence!"

"Maybe you should just watch where you're going," Terrance said.

Kusme turned. He looked as if he'd forgotten the janitor was there. His eyes were wide, his hair disheveled and his crisp blue suit, which had probably been worth more than Terrance's house, was ripped at the sleeve. "What did you just say?"

"I said maybe you should watch where you're going. It would probably be cheaper."

It was clear that the billionaire wasn't used to anyone talking to him like that — certainly not a lowly custodian—but Terrance didn't care. He'd almost died saving this asshole, and for what? Guys like him never thought twice about people like Terrance.

He was already trying to figure out how he was going to explain losing his job to Maria when Kusme burst out laughing.

"He has a point, no? I have a 143 IQ. I should probably know enough to look both ways." He clapped Terrance on the shoulder. "What's your name floor sweeper?"

"Terrance Meeks."

"Meeks, eh? Thank you. Thank you, Meeks."

He shook the custodian's hand and then walked away, leaving Terrance flabbergasted, but grateful to still have a job. He sat at the bus stop afterward, trying to process what just happened. It didn't seem real, even as his shoulder ached in testimony of the fall. Then he went home and told his wife about his daring rescue of the world-famous tycoon. She told him he should have asked for a reward.

"A man like that spends enough on dinner to put Trina through college," she said. "A good man like you should get something for saving him.

Terrance hadn't thought about that. She was probably right. She almost always was. It would have hurt his pride to ask for money, but no more than years of scrubbing piss and mud. And what was his pride next to his daughter's future? A college degree might just be a piece of paper to some, but Terrance knew that it would be obvious which weighs more if you put a diploma on one side of a scale and pride on the other.

He spent weeks beating himself up for his missed opportunity, certain that he'd never see or hear from Erik Kusme again. Then he got a letter in the mail. The envelope was made of heavy woven parchment and the return address, which said "From the Office of Erik Kusme," was written in flowing calligraphy. Terrance ripped it open from the corner and yanked out a letter that was penned in the same fashion.

Dear Mr. Meeks,

It occurs to me that I never properly thanked you for saving my life. I'm a very busy man. That's no excuse for rudeness, but it can make scheduling amends problematic. I want you to know that I didn't forget what you did for me. I'm sure dying on the windshield of a car I designed would make for a dramatic end to my biography, but there is still much for me to do and frankly, I don't have time to die. I don't know how informed you are on the New Jerusalem project, but we're now selecting candidates for the first crop of settlers. It is an entirely self-sustaining, solar-powered space station. Most of the people selected will be scientists, engineers, and the odd artist to keep the liberal goons off my back. Only the best are being allowed entry, but someone's going to have to keep the place clean. I am hereby granting you and your family a place on the station. Pay is 200K a year. Think it over.

-Sir Erik Kusme, CTO ZX Enterprises

PS: I'm doing my best to watch where I'm going.

Terrance showed the letter to Maria. First, she cried. Then she hugged him. Then she went back to crying. A half-hour later, she seemed to have gotten most of it out of her system. She was sitting on the couch with a cigarette in her hand.

It wasn't lit. They'd both quit the minute they found out she was pregnant. She just liked the feel of the filter on her lips, the texture of the paper between her fingers. Terrance didn't like that she kept them around. The smell of tobacco made his whole body itch.

"We're going to go up in the rocket?" she asked. Her voice shook.

"Seems like it," Terrance said. His leg was starting to bruise from where he kept pinching himself in his pocket.

"Does the letter say when?"

"I... I don't know."

He pulled it out and read it over again. It didn't give him any information at all. He didn't know when they'd be leaving or what they were expected to do in the meantime. Would they have to get trained as astronauts? Terrance had gotten a D- in high school science. He didn't think he was astronaut material.

"It doesn't say anything," he told her. "I guess they'll contact us?"

She snorted. "Rich people."

It was two days before Terrance heard from ZX Enterprises. He was starting to think the whole thing was a practical joke. He'd bragged to anyone who'd listen about saving Erik Kusme's life. Maybe one of his bar friends thought it would be funny to watch him mouth off about going to space.

Then a man in a suit showed up at his door. He explained that if they were going, it would need to be within the month. They wouldn't need astronaut training. They would, however, need to sign a minimum twenty-year contract. Shipping people back and forth from space wasn't cheap and ZX needed to make sure they were getting their money's worth. New Jerusalem was intended to be a colony after all. Ideally, most of the colonists would decide to live their entire lives up there.

They told the man about Maria's pregnancy. He said the company has already looked into both of their medical histories and that there were no problems.

"In fact," he said. "Mr. Kusme has personally expressed his excitement upon learning the child of the man who saved him would be among the first to be born in space. Once you're on board, you'll have access to some of the best OB/GYNs in the world, or off it in this case."

Maria started crying again, but they took the offer. Twenty years was a long time, but they'd be millionaires by the end and their daughter could live whatever life she wanted. Terrance thanked the man in the suit and showed him out.

"Our child will be born up there," his wife said, her eyes fixed on the bulge in her stomach that was just starting to show. "She'll be born up there and she'll be a woman before she ever comes back. She might never meet her Abuela."

On the station, they used a solution of concentrated white vinegar and some sort of lab-grown enzyme. It was extremely pungent and he had to scrub everything twice as hard, not least because of the slightly lower gravity. The people in charge chose the compound for two reasons. First, they could make it on-site which was important because everything in New Jerusalem had to be sustainable, and second, because the substance was completely non-toxic. You could lick any floor on the station and come away perfectly healthy, though Terrance probably wouldn't recommend it.

They'd been up there seventeen years now. Terrance had watched his little girl grow up into a brilliant, strong-willed woman like her mother. Trina was in her senior year at the station academy. She had spent the last night crying because she was third from valedictorian.

"I just wanted to impress you," she said through muffled sobs. "I wanted you to be able to rub it in all those snobs' faces."

"You're too hard on yourself," he said, running his chemically scarred fingers through locks of silky black hair. "New Jerusalem is full of geniuses, but not everything that makes you smart is measured in tests. You're the smartest person I've ever met, and I once met the guy who built this place."

"Oh, did you?" she asked, her voice saturated with sarcasm. "I don't think I remember the first million times you told me."

"My point is that I am proud of you. I don't need to rub anything in anyone's face. I pity them for not having a daughter like you. It's your mother who likes to gloat."

Maria had done very well for herself since coming to the station as well. She started as a maid, cleaning the houses of the wealthier residents on the station, but she got a job helping the botanists tend the greenhouses after less than a year. She couldn't recite the Latin names of every plant or classify each of them by genus and sub-genus, but she knew how to compost and that was a necessary job that no one else seemed keen on. Having her in charge of it left the brains free to experiment with zero gravity plant sex or whatever else they thought was more pressing of their time.

Terrance was still cleaning floors though. When he was pushing his mop, he might as well have been in any other building. The linoleum up here wasn't anything special.

Sometimes he listened to music while he worked. Other times he liked the quiet; when there was nothing but his thoughts and the slap of wet cotton on the floor. People could be rude, and they often were, but Terrance never questioned the value of his work. He enjoyed knowing that he left everything a little cleaner than it was before he came through.

Midway through his shift, he liked to sit on a bench that faced the solar windows in the bio-dome park. If he worked slow and took his break late, the sun would be behind him and the Earth would be glowing at the bottom of the window, just under his feet. His daughter used to come sit with him when she was younger and he would feed her slices of his apple while telling stories of his life down there, but it had been a long time since that last happened. Now he ate his food in silence.

It was on a day like this when Terrance saw the world end. He was sitting on his bench, eating what he was pretending was a pulled pork sandwich, and looking at that beautiful blue ball. He'd been studying his daughter's maps of the world and liked to play a game with himself where he would try to see how many of the countries he could identify by their geography. He was tracing the mountain ranges of Georgia when hundreds of bursts of white light sprang up across the planet's surface. He ran to the window and pressed his palms against the freshly cleaned glass, but there was nothing he could do. He watched helplessly as the sparks of light burst, plumed, and then receded into black marks against the green and gray.

He would later learn that the armistice between the United States and the New Soviet Union failed. The two superpowers had finally done what they'd been beating their chests about since the earlier half of the twenty-first century. No one knew who fired first. No one much cared. The titans trampled the Earth beneath their warring feet.

His brain struggled to grasp the scope of what he was seeing. He tried to think about five thousand years of human civilization coming to an end, but the idea was too big. It meant nothing to him. So instead, he tried thinking about the nine and a half billion people living down there, but that might as well have been the same thing. He narrowed the tragedy until he found something he could wrap his mind around.

He thought about his social worker, Pete, who'd never stopped trying to find him a home, even when he was too old to be adopted. He thought about the kids who stole his vodka, though they'd all be adults by now, and the principal who'd fired him. He pictured the old hotel manager and the prostitutes who used to wink at him whenever they left their tricks. He thought about the genius, Erik Kusme. He thought about his daughter's abuela, who fought through cancer to stay alive long enough to meet her granddaughter but was dead now just the same.

Terrance could wrap his mind around these people, and the grief choked him. He sobbed harder than he had ever sobbed; harder than when lye had melted the skin off his neck. Even harder than he had cried when Trina was born. It took a long time for him to regain control of himself.

His hands searched for the comfort of his mop. The handle was made of birch, he thought, or some other light wood. It was grown on Earth. It felt good, rubbing in its familiar way against his calluses. He put his nose to the ground and started mopping as alarms sounded throughout the station. People started to scramble to the windows so they could watch as the world ended, but Terrance continued to push his mop, cleaning the only mess under his power.

New Eyes

I was thirteen years old when we lost the color blue. I'd been warming up for a little league game by playing catch with my friend Sasha. She was winding her arm up to give me a pop-fly when there was a flash of white and everything changed. I thought there might have been something wrong with my eyes at first. Maybe a blood vessel had burst as I tracked the ball's path across the sun, coating my pupil in blood. That might have explained why the world was suddenly drowning in hues of orange, yellow, and undiluted red.

The ball landed softly in the grass, its lush green blades now looking dead and dry.

I struggled to think of a reason for the shift in color; as if knowing why everything suddenly looked so different would somehow make the change easier to process. I'd just learned about supervolcanoes in school. I wondered if the ash that was supposed to bury us in decades of darkness could be responsible for the sudden shift in color.

The adults were the first to scream. Only afterward did the kids start crying. Only once they were certain what was happening to them could not simply be blinked away. I looked around and felt this new, sallow field starting to spin.

Sasha rushed over and grabbed my hands.

"Do you smell that?" she asked.

I sniffed the air, wondering if she had picked up the acrid stench of sulfur, but I didn't smell anything. She smiled as I inhaled the perfectly ordinary oxygen.

"Just keep breathing," she said. "Panicking won't help anything."

Sasha would later tell me that her mom had severe anxiety. Panic attacks were a common occurrence for her. Maybe that was why she was so calm. She already had more practice than most adults at holding everything together while her world fell apart.

A lot of scientists believed that something happened to the sun at first. They thought that some sort of cosmic event must have occurred that caused our star to no longer emit blue light. There are other sources of light besides the sun though. They quickly disproved this theory with a simple LED bulb. The blue light was still there. Our eyes had simply lost the ability to perceive it.

But as greater minds struggled over the why and how of the phenomenon, the rest of us were forced to adapt to our new reality. It wasn't just Picasso's formative collection that was lost. A whole third of the spectrum had vanished. Every shade of purple, green, and even brown had disappeared along with the blue. Yet the president came on the news after only a few weeks of hunkering down in our homes and thinking that the world was at its end. He made it clear the loss of a single prime color was no excuse to shut down society.

Our parents went back to work, and they still expected us to go to school. I learned about the vibrant ecology that existed beneath the beige surface of the ocean in Science. I squeezed amber acrylic from a tube to paint sepia tones in Art. I read about the once verdant green forests surrounding Walden Pond in Literature. I used to hate Math before the shift, but I found comfort in it afterward. It seemed to be the only thing that hadn't changed.

Sometimes I came home to find my mother crying with her face pressed into the crimson curtains hanging in our living room. Purple had been her favorite color.

I ended up dating Sasha in high school until she broke up with me for being too self-absorbed—which I was. Then I left home, went to college in Boston, and got my degree. I eventually got a job modeling hydraulic construction for civil water resources—a fancy way of saying I designed pipes and drains for the city. That might sound boring to some people, but I enjoyed it. There was an art to creating systems that could mesh into the historic city's twisting blocks and archaic waterways. I didn't stay long though. I moved back home when the doctors diagnosed my dad with emphysema.

"It's all the yellow," he said. "It's impossible to breathe with all this yellow."

I suspected it had more to do with the pack of Marlboro Reds he kept hidden in the woodshed that my mom pretended not to know about.

Sasha reached out to me when she heard I was back in town. We met up at a dive bar called The Blue Lantern. We downed cheap beer from a plastic pitcher and reminisced about how glamorous we'd imagined drinking there would be when we were in high school.

Once the pitcher was empty, she took me by the hand and led me to her loft down the street. We smoked, listened to music, and then had sex on her rose-patterned comforter. I felt her fingers tickling over my stomach as we lay in the sweat-soaked bed afterward, our chests heaving in the darkness.

"Sometimes I can still see it," she said.

"See what?"

"Blue. Sometimes after a few drinks and a good fuck, I close my eyes and I can still see the world the way it used to be."

"Did you see it just now, with me?" I asked.

"No," she said, and I felt her drag her teeth across the skin on my shoulder, "but I'm willing to try again."

We got married that spring. We danced, ate cake, and spent precious time with those we loved. Our families shared a few stories from our youthful years on the pitch—of azure skies, spring green fields, and royal purple uniforms. It was good to remember, but we mostly celebrated the life ahead and tried not to dwell on the one left behind.

We eventually bought a house. It was a burnt orange bungalow that had a cherry tree in the back. I hated the way abandoned fruit fell to the ground and stained the pavement with its bloody red pulp. No matter how diligently we raked, a few pungent pieces always slipped through and fermented in the summer sun. But Sasha loved them, and I loved her.

I was collecting the cherries in a bowl when she raced out of the house to tell me we were pregnant. We celebrated, calling our friends and loved ones to tell them the good news. I smiled at Sasha and told her how happy I was. Though later that night, when the lights were out and I could hear her breathing soften as she drifted into sleep, I secretly mourned that my child would never see the vibrant splendor of the world as I had.

That dread lingered until the doctor handed my daughter to me. She was 7lbs, 3oz of fragile bones covered in soft fat and raw, pink flesh. She cried and wriggled her tiny limbs with reckless, audacious life. Her gaze was hungry and wild. She wanted to see everything. She was so eager to be a part of this red land; this blueless Earth.

Something changed in me as I held her. For the first time I could remember, I wasn't yearning for a past that would never return. I was back in a world of true color as I saw everything through her perfect, new eyes.

ONLY HUMAN

I wonder about the dreaming dead.
   Their lonely fears,
   their warm ambitions,
   the lust that made their blankets stretch.

I think about their children's children.
   Their early summers,
   their elder winters,
   the seconds when life made sense.

It hurts to know I'm just like them.
   With short breaths,
   and long sleep,
   watching seconds tick like a gavel.

I wish, but no.
I want, but no.
Immortality is unoriginal.

GLAMOUR

The mistress would visit her husband's grave tonight. He wasn't her favorite husband, merely her most recent. Still, she had loved him and love was never an easy thing to lose.

I was still getting her breakfast ready when she came down the stairs, effervescent in black, as only she could be. She wore a broad hat with a midnight veil stitched to its brim. It was the type of fashion that must have been popular in her youth—or at least, a time when youth was still in more recent memory.

I held my breath when she entered certain rooms. The light seemed to pass through her at times, allowing her cold beauty to shine like a dying star.

The boy I prepared for her was still writhing against his bonds. The knots were all tied correctly and the hook had held the weight of men three times his size, but it was still quite annoying. His squirming shook dust loose from the ceiling, which settled on my freshly cleaned counters.

I wondered if I somehow got the dosage wrong for the sedative. It's happened before, though not for a long time. It was a delicate balance, after all. Too much could prove fatal.

But I couldn't help but wonder if that was all there was to it. Could it be possible that I miscalculated on purpose? Perhaps there was some part of me that subconsciously wanted him to escape. Mistress would have to chase him down if he did. She would hunt him through the streets of Jamestown like a raptor seeking a rodent. She'd beat me for letting him go, but the thrill of an old-fashioned hunt might have distracted her from her grief.

A tear rolled down the boy's cheek as he finally stopped squirming. The tranquilizer must have won in the end. I suppose he just had a bit more fight in him than most.

"Good evening, Mistress. Will you be drinking from the source today, or would you prefer a glass?"

"I'm not thirsty tonight, Millie," she said, pain etched deep in her voice.

"But you need your strength. Mr. Solomon wouldn't want you collapsing from hunger, would he?"

She looked at me, pleading.

I wished that I could take the hurt out of her. She was so pure and innocent. It was like watching a child fall and scrape their knee for the first time.

She'd lost husbands before, I knew, and I wondered if it was like this every time. She loved too fiercely, felt too deeply, and despair would creep into her like a cancer when that love was gone. I wanted her to know that I would soak her pain into myself if I could, leaving nothing in her but joy and carelessness. I didn't have that power, though. All I could do was hold her gaze.

"A glass then," she sighed, defeated.

I fixed the bleeding collar around the boy's neck. It had a small stainless-steel tap fixed on the side of it, not unlike those used on maple trees to collect syrup. I picked up the little wooden mallet I kept with the dinnerware and gently used it to tap in the needle and puncture the boy's carotid. Then I readied a glass beneath the spout so as not to make a mess of the freshly scrubbed floor.

"Would you like the car, or would you prefer to walk to the cemetery?" I asked her as the vibrant, arterial blood flowed into the glass.

"I'll walk, I think."

I removed the glass from the tap when it was three-quarters full and connected a vinyl tube in its place. It led to a cask in the refrigerator, which would preserve the rest of the boy's blood for later.

I gave the mistress her glass and watched as she sipped delicately from the crystal. Liquid ruby etched its way through the grooves in her pale lips. If you watched carefully, you could see the color rise to her cheeks ever so slightly. She usually savored the drink, especially a vintage as young and vibrant as this one, but today her mind was far away. Her eyes appeared to gaze through the eastern wall toward the stable where her husband had collapsed after his evening ride. Heart failure, the doctor had said. Perfectly natural. Perfectly human.

I went to the hutch by the door when she was finished to gather her evening coat and walking stick. The night was temperate and the walk up the cobbled path wasn't far, but the last thing I wanted was for the evening wind to cause her any discomfort.

I helped her arms into the sleeves before we headed out into the early night. There was still the faintest hue of orange twinging the western sky. Winter was coming to a close, and the sun was setting later as spring breathed new life into the earth. At least my lady would have her garden again soon. Perhaps tending to her herbs and flowers would distract her.

The moon was little more than half full as we passed the gate. Its light cast eerie silhouettes through the barren trees as the path steadily curved upward. The top of the hill neighboring my lady's house had the plot where her husband was buried. Graveyards were always built that way here. Otherwise, the town would run the risk of bodies washing up during the winter floods. The ground in the valley had just begun to thaw into icy mud, but the soil on the hill held firm—all but the freshly churned earth over Francis Solomon's grave.

My mistress dropped to her knees then, her porcelain face suddenly full of lines as anguish overwhelmed her. Knowing it wasn't my place, I nevertheless crouched to my knees and put my arms around her shoulders. We sat in silence like that for a long time. I listened as the wind whispered over wet grass and watched as storm clouds traced their blackness across the star-strewn violet blue.

"He was a good man, wasn't he, Millie?" Mistress asked, speaking for what must have been the first time in hours. Her voice was tight from misuse, and yet it still sounded like a song.

"Yes Mistress, he was."

"He grew up here in town, you know. I knew him when he was a boy. He was never afraid of me like the others. He used to sneak into my stables and feed apples to the horses. I caught him once. Did I ever tell you about that?"

"Yes, Mistress."

"I thought about keeping him, of course. It's hard not to when they wander in on their own, but there was something in that stubbornness that I liked about him, something sweet too. I let him go, but I would smell apples on the horses' breath every once in a while and know he'd been back.

"Eventually, I left him a note saying that he may as well take a job tending to them in the evenings if he liked them so much. I knew his family needed the money. I remember the way he used to hum as he brushed them. It was an old tune. It surprised me that anyone else still knew it. Then all the boys went to Vietnam, and I realized I was afraid I might never hear it again. It was a curious thing to feel over a town boy. That was when I realized I must have loved him. I decided that I would marry him if he survived."

"That's beautiful," I said.

"I don't think I ever told you about his nightmares, though, did I? This was before your time. He used to wake up in the middle of the day screaming and drenched in sweat. It broke my heart to see him like that. He begged me to take the nightmares away. I could have done it, of course, but then he would have been just another puppet. I didn't want to do that to him. I wanted Francis to stay Francis, no matter what."

"So, what happened?"

"Nothing, really. The dreams became less frequent over time. He still had them, even to the end, but they were less intense. He would wake up hearing the screams, just like always, but he eventually stopped screaming with them."

I remembered a few late nights when I heard the creak of footsteps outside my door and peeked through the gap to see Mr. Solomon shuffling toward the entryway. I'd assumed he was sleepwalking, but maybe he was seeking a comfortable place to ride out the day where his ghosts wouldn't disturb his sleeping wife.

"He was so gentile," Mistress moaned. "Nothing like my last husband. Ryan was an oil baron. Everything about him exuded entitlement. I confess it was the quality I initially found most attractive about him. A man who felt the whole world belonged to him seemed a natural match for me at the time. The only problem was that Ryan didn't know where the line was drawn. He occasionally had the misconception that I belonged to him as well. It was truly unfortunate when I had to eat him. In truth, the experience put me off men for a while."

"What about the one before Ryan?" I asked. "The inventor. What was his name?" I'd heard these stories many times, but my lady's voice was starting to even as she lost herself in memory.

"Elias?" she laughed. "I suppose he was an inventor of sorts. He was the one who convinced me to have electricity installed in the house. It was considered something of a base luxury at the time, but you can't imagine what it was like for one such as I to suddenly re-enter a world of light. Elias spent his life trying to come up with something to rival it. He failed, but I admired his drive. He did create my bleeding collar. The device's utility was unique to my needs, but it was quite elegant. Before that, the servants used to just slit their throats over a bucket. You can't imagine the mess."

She was nearly smiling now. I wanted to keep her going.

"Before him, you were married to a lord, no?"

She looked at me. Her eyes suddenly grew sharp beneath her veil, and I knew she saw right through my ploy.

"Three lords, a silk trader, a shipwright, and a pig farmer. Do you enjoy hearing me list out my collection?" she asked, her voice suddenly acid. "Are you impressed with their variety?"

"I'm sorry, Mistress," I said, bowing my head.

She turned back to the gravestone.

"I suppose it's natural for you to be curious, but you must understand that there is no respite from grief to be found in memory. Past love cannot erase fresh loss, nor the bitterness of being alone."

The wind picked up to fill the gap in conversation. A cloud passed before the moon and my lady became a wraith against the night. Her shroud was a wisp, barely perceptible as it billowed in the violet-black. My heart ached to tell her she wasn't alone, but even *I* didn't have that much audacity. Instead, I stood sentinel to her grief.

"I've been thinking of dying," Mistress said suddenly.

Then the wind stopped, leaving us in a sudden, buzzing silence.

"You can't, mistress," I said, horrified at the thought.

"It is difficult, but I assure you, it can be done."

"You know what I mean," I said, suddenly angry. I'd never been angry at her before. It was a confusing feeling. "Please don't even talk about such a dreadful thing."

"Do you remember when I killed your mother, Millie?" she asked.

I saw a flash of auburn hair, a woman singing show tunes as she stocked aisles in a grocery store. I smelled the scent of cloves in a warm hug. Then there was blood spurting everywhere, a scream, and a profound sense of anguish melting away, like tingling nerves dissolving in a warm bath."

"I remember," I said.

"She was pretty. You were a stick of a thing when I took you, but you're starting to look like her now."

"Please, Mistress. I don't want to talk about this."

"Ah, but it isn't up to you. I am your mistress. So I will talk about ripping your mother's throat out if I want to, and I'll talk about ending my life if it pleases me. Your role is to listen and obey."

"I'm sorry Mistress. It was selfish of me. I just don't want to think of a world without you."

"That's enough," said another voice from the night.

A lantern clicked on near the tree line on the bank of the hill. Then a woman stepped forward, her face lit up in the orange, propane-fueled flame. She wore a large flannel coat over sweats and boots. It looked like she'd come from bed. Her eyes were a latticework of red veins and her cheeks were smeared with the beaded black of runny eyeliner.

"I've been listening," the woman said. "I heard what you said about all your different husbands. I heard what you said about the girl's mom. I'd heard the rumors about you—and God help me, I didn't believe them—but I heard you say you can die just now and I suppose that's all I need to know."

"Are you going to introduce yourself, then?" Mistress asked the woman.

"Does it matter?"

My blood boiled at her rudeness. My hand moved to the knife I kept stashed in the hem of my skirt, but my lady held out her arm, gesturing for me to be still. I obeyed.

"Indulge me," Mistress said to her.

"My name is Brianne Collins. I own a farm just outside town. My son's name was Joshua. I got a call from him, but all I could hear was the two of you talking about visiting a cemetery. I found my boy hanging from that meat hook you got in your kitchen with a tube sticking out of his neck. I pulled him down, but his body was already cold. So, I came here."

Her voice sounded weak, wrong somehow. It wasn't just sorrow that made it waver like that. I didn't like it.

"Are you expecting an apology?" Mistress asked.

"I don't know," the Collins woman said, her legs shaking. "I thought you were just an animal, but now I see you mourning your husband. That makes it worse somehow. At least an animal doesn't know any better."

I knew Mistress was fast. I'd seen her flit through Jamestown like a bird of prey when her quarry was loose in the streets. She dropped her walking stick and was across the yard before it had time to hit the ground. I wasn't expecting the Collins woman to be fast too, though. A shotgun appeared from beneath her coat and a blast echoed through the valley that sent sleeping birds scattering into the night. The woman fumbled through her coat pocket and pulled out another shell. I ran towards her, knife drawn, but my mistress was faster. She was off the ground and had her fangs in the Collins woman's neck before she had time to open the chamber.

It was over. There was a moment where the only sound was the mistress as she gulped greedily from the woman's neck. She would drain her dry, just like I did to her son. Then the blood would course through her and heal that wound like new. The Collins woman achieved nothing. It made me sad, though I didn't understand why.

Then Mistress made a loud choking sound and detached her fangs. She coughed and a gush of red mist shot from between her beautiful lips. "What did you do, you stupid cow?" she asked.

The woman laughed. It was an ugly, guttural sound, made worse by the blood oozing from the corner of her mouth.

"I found your stash," she burbled, and I suddenly remembered the vials of horse tranquilizer that had been in the refrigerator beside the cask for storing blood. "Drank three bottles right before I stepped out to say hello. Wasn't sure if it would work on a thing like you. Glad to know..." but then her voice trailed off to nothing.

Mistress turned to look at me. Black veins were tracing their way up her pale cheeks. There was something wild in her eyes, something I'd never seen before, and I felt genuine fear for the first time since the day my mother died.

"I'm sorry. It seems I was wrong," she said, loping towards me. All affectations of grace were gone now. She moved like an injured wolf, slow and jagged, but all the more dangerous. "I'm not ready to die just yet."

Panic coursed through me, though I wasn't sure why. It should have been my dream to die for the mistress. I'd spent so many nights praying that I might eventually feel the cool oblivion of her lips as my blood became a part of her. So why were my legs shaking?

I took a step backward and tripped over a low headstone. Something loud snapped under the weight of my body.

"Wait," I said. "Something isn't right."

"The glamour is fading," she replied, still stumbling forward. "It's a shame. I would have wished for you to die loving me."

I reached behind me and my fingers wrapped around something smooth and light. I clamped my eyes shut and swung it around just as Mistress lunged at me, desperate to put anything between my neck and her fangs. I felt a blow as something heavy hit me in the gut, and then hot liquid splashed over my hands and chest. I opened my eyes and realized that the thing I had grabbed was the mistress's broken walking stick. Its jagged edge was now thrust between her ribs. Her wretched face was frozen in shock, and I wondered how I ever thought she was beautiful.

"Sorry Mistress," I said. "I'm not ready to die either."

I pushed her body off of me and struggled to my feet. Everything I'd done for the last eleven years came surging back. I replayed all the times that I watched in awe as that creature used her teeth to tear into the throats of her victims. I saw the panicked eyes of those who pleaded with me to spare them as I drove the spiked collar into their necks. I remembered my mother mouthing for me to run as the color leeched out of her face.

A decade of suppressed guilt surged through me like a maelstrom. I felt as though I couldn't breathe. My heart hammered and the veins in my temples felt like they were about to burst. Then, just as the pressure in my head reached its zenith, I vomited.

I forced myself to walk over to Brianne Collins when the night finally stopped spinning. I rolled her onto her back so that her eyes faced the stars. Her face was still, her mouth etched in a bitter grin. I couldn't ask her forgiveness for what I'd done to her son, but I said a quiet prayer of thanks. At least there wouldn't be any more blood on my hands. I wished there were words to make any of this right, but there was nothing. Without anywhere else to go, I walked out of the cemetery and back to the manor. I'd figure out what to do next in the morning.

Here and Gone

It was a bleak December morning when the deliverymen dropped off the machine. It took three of them to get it through the door. The one who asked for my signature was a heavyset man with a mustache. The others called him Gabe. His breath smelled of wintergreen that didn't quite mask the spice of bourbon. I took the clipboard and scrawled an illegible line across the bottom. I used to have a tidy signature where you could actually read my name, but my hand was numb by the time I finished my second book tour.

The deliverymen used a box cutter to strip away the cardboard casing until it fell away, revealing what looked like an old-timey photo booth with three sturdy walls and a maroon curtain.

I shook their hands and offered them a few extra dollars for their effort. My mother was a server for most of her life and she taught me to always tip people who have to deal with the public, even if it's only a dollar or two. I don't know if my pocket change has ever brightened anyone's day, but I might have been able to put a kid through college if you added it all together.

"Thanks," Gabe said. "Enjoy the teleporter."

Then they left, sealing the door behind them. The house was quiet now they were gone. I could once again hear the constant ambient vibration of San Francisco's traffic. I usually tuned it out the way you would a ticking clock, but it often broke through in the early seconds of silence, humming in the walls like loose plumbing.

I didn't like the black-painted wooden box the men delivered. It was obtrusive. Its panels jutted from the wall beyond the sofa, demanding attention. The word 'Telepro' was printed on the side in gold-leaf lettering. I took a moment to look over its considerable dimensions before poking my head inside.

The curtain was heavy, like the lead-lined bib they used to make you wear to get your teeth x-rayed. The inside of the box looked alien in its complexity. It was all metal, gears, glass, and wires. It was tight and uncomfortable with a hundred probing mechanical eyes all staring at its center, making it hard to blink. Looking at it made my skin itch, so I stalked out of the living room and back to my office.

Steph and I bought a two-bedroom in case we ever had a child. The second room became my study after the miscarriage, though. It was a tight space, like all extra rooms in the city, but it was cozy. I lined the walls with shelves of well-worn books that covered the circus animal wallpaper. The desk I'd picked up back in college was crammed in the corner. It was an old wooden thing with drawers that swelled shut in the warm months. It was the same desk where I wrote my first published story and the same desk where Stephanie and I made love for the first time. Like all first times, it was mindlessly passionate and horribly uncomfortable. I'm pretty sure a loose paper clip stabbed me in the thigh at one point.

It was also the only room where Steph let me smoke. My dad's pipe was leaning against an ashtray beside my old Remington Royal. The polished cherry wood bit was pockmarked from years of frustrated gnawing and the inside was charred black despite hundreds of cleanings. I put it in my mouth and sat down at the freshly oiled typewriter to work on my newest novel.

It didn't have a title yet. It didn't even have a proper outline. Right now, it was just an idea for a character and a few pages about the firehouse where he spent most of his childhood. I'd called him Gary as a placeholder, but I still wasn't completely sold on the name. Smirking to myself, I toyed with the idea of changing it to Gabe as I packed the tobacco into my pipe. There wasn't much left in the tin. I'd have to go to the shop soon. Staring at the page, I re-read the last lines I'd written six times before touching the keys.

"After school, Gary went straight to Station 15. He did his homework in the den and watched the men of the department eat sandwiches, never knowing if five minutes later they'd be dealing a few hands of rummy or running into an inferno."

I tried to put myself in Gary's prepubescent mind. I breathed smoke into my lungs and tried to imagine myself as someone small, surrounded by heroes. It didn't work. All I could think about was that damn box in my living room. I closed my eyes and imagined myself in the warm laughter and bustle of the firehouse, but all I saw were cold metal rods and mechanical glass eyes staring back.

I gave up after a fruitless hour, smothering my pipe but leaving it in my mouth so I could still taste it. I decided to go into the kitchen and make myself a cup of coffee instead. I heard the front door open as the pot was heating. There was a familiar clamor of bags being unloaded and the kicking off of wood-heeled shoes.

"Is it here?" came Steph's voice. I heard her moving into the living room. I poked my head out to see her leaning through the maroon curtain. "Neat," she said. "It's just like the one we have at work. Have you tried it yet?"

"Hell no. I don't think you should, either."

She popped back out and gave me one of her old standbys, a smirk that said *I love you, but you know you're being ridiculous.*

A few strands of bright copper came loose from the knot she had her hair in. I hated how she could be so beautiful and so condescending at the same time.

"Arnie, we'd never even use the dishwasher if you had your way. The Telepro is bought and paid for. We can't just not use it."

"We certainly can. I told you not to buy it."

"Yes, but I did it with my money, so you have no say in the matter."

I felt my hands tighten, but I didn't want to fight. I took a deep breath before responding. "We can still send it back. You already have a car. I don't see why you need this thing, anyway."

"You'd feel differently if you spent as much time in traffic as I do."

"Well, shouldn't we at least test it?" I asked. "How do we even know it works? What if this one's defective?"

She cocked an eyebrow, still wearing that smile, and walked over to me. She put an arm around my neck and plucked the pipe from my lips in order to plant a soft kiss. I could feel her body pressed against me, warm and lithe beneath her winter clothes.

This is how she gets away with it, I thought to myself. *She does whatever she wants and you just let her.*

But I was on cloud nine by the time she pulled away. Kissing Steph made an adolescent light bloom inside me, blinding me to everything else. She knew about the power she had over me, and frequently used it to her advantage. I'd all but forgotten about the machine when she walked away and stuck my pipe behind the curtain. I moaned when I realized what she was doing, too late to stop her from sending it.

"Call Janet," she said. The monitor on the wall clicked on and suddenly we were looking through a window into Janet Smith's house. It was bigger than ours, an old Victorian her aunt gave her after Janet had her second baby. The woman herself stood in the middle of the vaulted living room, wearing a pantsuit and a pair of fluffy pink slippers. Janet never did anything to make me dislike her, but sometimes I hated lucky people on principle.

"Oh good. You got it!" she exclaimed, looking over Steph's shoulder at the machine.

"Yup, it just showed up," Steph said, matching Janet's excitement. Then the volume of her voice lowered as if she were whispering a joke that only the two of them were allowed to hear. "Arnold thinks it might not be safe. He wanted to test it, so I sent you his pipe. Would you mind sending it back to us so he can see that it's perfectly fine?"

"Oh, not at all," Janet chirped, walking over to her own black box. "Kinda funny if you ask me, him putting that poison in his lungs and accusing a Telepro of not being safe. I'll send it over now."

"Thanks, Janet," Steph said. Then she hung up the call.

The lights dimmed as the box came to life with a quiet whir, like a refrigerator clicking on.

"Big draw on the power," I said, trying to sound conversational.

"It's cheaper than gas," Steph replied.

The whirring stopped, and she reached behind the curtain, producing the pipe and handing it to me. It was cold to the touch, but otherwise appeared the same. The cherry shone in the lamplight. The inside appeared scorched from years of use. It even had the same tooth marks on the bit. I put it to my lips and I could still taste the Turkish tobacco I'd smoked earlier that evening.

"Please wait," I said, surprising myself with how desperate my voice sounded. "Just give me one day. Let me read up on it and try to get my head around the stupid thing. If I still can't convince you to get rid of it tomorrow night, then I won't say another word."

Steph looked at me like she wasn't sure if I was joking or not. Then the mocking smile fell, and she put her hand on my cheek.

"Alright," she said. "One day."

We had orange chicken and rice for dinner that night. Then we started watching a drama we liked. We were enjoying it until the punky girl with blue hair tearfully announced to her boyfriend that she was pregnant. I changed it to a show about unusual animals becoming friends. After that, we made love and fell asleep.

It was raining hard when Steph's alarm went off in the morning. I was doing my best to be the good husband, so I set about making breakfast as she dragged herself into the shower. I made bacon, eggs, and enough coffee to be certain she'd have a second cup. She cleaned her plate and even managed to groan a thank you before donning her rain gear and trudging out of the house.

I went back to the box once she was gone. There was a digital manual taped to the side. I peeled it off and sat on the couch to read about the monstrosity I'd allowed into my home.

'The Telepro maps every atom of whatever is placed inside,' it said. 'Clothes, money, a sense of humor—nothing is left behind! The machine transfers this information to another licensed Telepro device which then prints the material in milliseconds. For the first time ever, teleportation is fast, affordable, and above all, safe.'

Scrolling down to the bottom of the page, there was a quote beside a photograph of a darkly bearded man in a white lab coat. He looked like a cross between Allen Ginsberg and Victor Frankenstein.

"The hardest part was ensuring that memories were transferred properly. We've been able to 3D print organs and other solid matter for decades, but a brain is more than just its molecular makeup. It was like trying to map every volt in a storm."

I read it from top to bottom twice. Aside from the instructions, there was precious little information about how the machine actually worked. It claimed to be safer and more affordable than driving, but it didn't explain what it did with the old body once it was mapped, but before the new one was printed.

I thought about pages I'd Xeroxed, and how every copy I made lost something from the original. What might be lost here? I needed to make sure I articulated my fears to Steph. I had to make sure she understood why this machine made me so hesitant.

I went to my office and lit my pipe. Was I just being paranoid like Steph thought? The weight was identical. It had the same slick texture. The smoke came out in the same steady stream, seasoned by years of residue, but something about it just didn't sit right in the teeth. I knew it wasn't my father's pipe.

That didn't stop me from smoking it, though. At a certain point, the body starts to need nicotine more than sentiment.

I tried to research the Telepro on the computer, using one machine to discredit another. I didn't get much traction there, though. It seemed the scientific community was on Steph's side. One site argued that cells naturally replicate every seven days and speeding up the process did no measurable harm. The only groups that seemed to agree with me were the same religious zealots who were forever screeching that anything new might somehow sully the soul.

Without a way to move forward, I went back to my novel. It turned into a pretty successful afternoon from there. I made it through two chapters with a break for lunch. I could feel Gary's story starting to take shape, only I still didn't have an ending. It's important to know how you're going to end a story before you get too deep into it. Writing without a roadmap can get you lost along the way.

Gary's character arc was still in its infancy. I needed time to let him grow and develop so that he could start to feel human. I wanted things to go well for him, but I could already tell it wasn't going to be that kind of story.

The lights flickered as I was reading back a line I'd just written to check its structure. I looked out the window at the raging storm.

"This is why you use a typewriter," I said to myself with a smirk.

Then I heard a thump coming from the living room.

I jumped to my feet, the sudden realization of what'd happened propelling me to the front of the house.

My wife was standing in front of the machine. She was perfectly dry, with her rain gear slung over one arm.

"Don't start," she said, wearing that familiar smile. "I'm fine. Nothing went wrong, just like I said it wouldn't."

"You said you'd wait till tomorrow."

"I know," she said, "but have you looked outside? It's flooding out there. We're going to have to start gathering two of every animal soon. Half the roads are closed and people are driving like maniacs. Do you want me to die on the commute home just so you can pretend it's still the twentieth century?"

"I wanted you to keep your word! I wanted to get rid of that thing before either of us set foot inside it! I spent all day trying to figure out how to make you understand why I don't trust it!"

"This isn't the first time I've used one," she said. Her voice was quiet, solemn. It was the way mine sounded in confession as a child. She didn't break eye contact, though. I could tell by the way she stared me down that she'd been thinking about telling me this for a long time. "I've used a few of them. The one at Janet's and the one at work. Sometimes just to make a quick trip to the store before coming home. They're everywhere now."

I didn't have an answer to that. I just looked at her. I could feel the shock and disbelief spread across my face. I wanted to say something. I wanted to scream at her, but I couldn't grasp the words.

"You know, it's easy for you to be uppity about it, Arnie," she continued. "You just sit in this house with ghosts all day. You don't have to go out there. The real world moves forward. It won't wait for us."

I felt like I was sleeping next to a stranger that night.

She was lying on her side. Had she always slept like that? The more I thought about it, the more certain I was that Steph usually slept on her back. I listened to her breathing to see if I could hear the faint whistle that sometimes escaped her nose. I felt the bed to see if she was putting off the same amount of body heat. I even smelled her hair to discern if it still had that mild aroma of coconut it's carried ever since she switched to the shampoo she found during our honeymoon in Maui.

I couldn't be sure, though. Was it still her, or could I simply not tell the difference between the woman I loved and a copy?

Unable to fall asleep, I got out of bed and went to the living room window. I wanted my pipe, but I'd cleaned out my tin of tobacco that afternoon. The rain was falling in heavy sheets. It was the kind of rain that you hear about Florida getting around hurricane season. Lampposts reflected in the moving surface of the street, their lights dancing like fireflies. It was nothing like the dense mist and foggy drizzles that accented the San Francisco of my childhood. The water thudded relentlessly against the glass, making a sound I could feel in the back of my brain.

It reminded me of the day Steph and I lost our little boy, which didn't make sense, because that day had been in the heart of summer. Her water broke in the car on the way to her checkup. We thought that was a good sign, providence. I'd never been prouder of my wife than I was that day. She was amazing. She fought for hours, never once giving up.

I could feel us dying when the doctor pulled that blue thing from her. I couldn't let that happen. I held Steph in my arms for hours and we promised that we'd never blame each other. I told her that I would love her even more than I did before, and that I would hold her up when things felt hopeless. It was hard to say if I'd kept that promise.

The black machine was like a hole in the dimly lit room, a void of space that would consume everything. I thought about getting my old baseball bat out of the garage. I wanted to smash the box to kindling and burn the remains, but I knew deep down that wouldn't fix anything. I was tired of fighting. I felt like the oldest thing in a new world. My veins were gasping for nicotine. A fresh start was what I needed, a quick trip to the smoke shop and then a full night's rest.

I crawled beyond the red veil, into the machine. I could feel the cold eyes scanning me as it hummed to life and knew this was as far as this body would go. I thought about the bearded man in the lab coat and how he said memory was the hardest part for the machine to map. I hoped some memories wouldn't make the trip.

HANDS

The world was built by many hands

Hands swinging hammers,
Hands bearing swords,
Hands wielding chisels,
Hands bound in chord.

Hands lifting banners,
Hands that hold,
Hands that wither,
and grow old.

Hands that crack.
Skin that bleeds.
Crippled hands,
hiding their needs.

Broken hands, with a trembling cup,
Remembering when they held us up.

GHOSTS IN THE DRYWALL

I held up Dad's old hunting knife to show Lyle the slender shard of glass sticking to its edge. It was about the size of a long grain of wild rice, ending in a slender point. A smear of his blood held it to the blade like an adhesive.

"There," I said, releasing his wrist. "Got it."

"I never asked for your help, Billy," he whined, putting the finger in his mouth. His cheeks flared in and out as he sucked on the injured digit.

"You never need to, little brother."

I grabbed a length of cloth from the tool bag, handing it to Lyle and telling him to keep pressure on it to stop the bleeding. I looked up at what was left of the bulb he'd been trying to pull from the fixture in the dining room. Only a single jagged piece of glass was attached to the metal base. The rest was scattered across the floor like chips of ice.

"Let's call it a day," I said, wiping the blood off the knife before flipping the blade into its bone handle and putting it back in my pocket. "We can start up again in the morning."

"I'll grab a broom," he said, stepping gingerly across the field of sharp debris toward the kitchen.

I watched him go, trying to suppress the urge to follow him. I reminded myself that Lyle was an adult, and that I had to give him his space.

It seemed like the house should have been a mess when our parents left it to us. It should have been vandalized, with smashed furniture and broken windows littering the floor. The walls themselves should have been crumbling under their own weight. How could it be exactly the same? Shouldn't it show some sign that its owners of thirty years were dead? Everything looked fine, though. It was the parts you couldn't see that were the trouble.

A loud crash came from the kitchen a moment later, followed by the low howl of Lyle cursing. I rushed after the sound. Broken glass from the light bulb crunched under my boots. My brother was sitting on the kitchen floor, rubbing his head and muttering violently.

"What happened?" I asked, holding out my hand to help him up. "Are you okay?"

"I'm fine," he said, pushing my arm away and sitting stubbornly with his back against the cabinet under the sink. "I tried to grab the broom off the hook, and Mom's stupid stock pot fell from the cupboard."

I looked across the floor where the giant stainless steel pot was gently rolling back and forth between its handles like a seesaw. The thing must have weighed at least eight pounds.

"Are you sure you're alright? You could have a concussion."

"Do you need me to walk a straight line, officer?" he asked, showing the edges of his teeth as he smiled. He liked to remind me how little he respected my job at the Sheriff's Department whenever he thought I was overstepping. "I told you I'm fine. Back off, alright?"

"Well, now I kind of wish you were concussed. Maybe that pot would've knocked out whatever part of your brain makes you such a little shit. When did you get so clumsy, anyway?"

"I don't know. I should never have come back to this stupid house."

I knew how he felt. I was starting to think the same thing, truth be told. The place looked just like it always had, but everything under the surface was rotten. The insulation was full of mold, the electrical was a rat-nested nightmare, and most of the plumbing had nearly eroded clean through. We'd been working on it the last few days between funeral preparations. I thought the project would be a good distraction and that it would make it easier for me to keep an eye on Lyle, but every problem we fixed seemed to reveal a dozen new things that needed attention. Our parents left it to us in their will, though it was starting to feel less like a gift and more like a punishment.

"Why don't you take it easy for a minute," I told him, grabbing the broom from where he'd dropped it on the floor. "I'll clean up the glass."

I swept the shards into a paper bag and threw them in the trash. Then the two of us sat down to eat a couple of microwave dinners and watch some TV in the living room. It was an old box tube since Dad refused to acknowledge that we'd moved into the twenty-first century. I wasn't watching the show so much as I was watching Lyle, though.

He was sitting in Dad's old La-Z-Boy recliner—the one we weren't allowed to touch as kids. He was picking through his food and occasionally taking a small bite of the molten brownie. It was strange being in that room without Mom or Dad. It felt like we were visiting, but no one was home.

We went into their room later that evening to choose clothes for them to be buried in. I'd been putting it off, but the funeral manager called and told us he needed them by tomorrow. I opened up Dad's closet and pulled out his best blue suit. It was pressed and clean, except for the faintest discoloration on the right cuff where he'd tried to staunch a persistent nosebleed at their vow renewal. He told me in confidence that he got them sometimes when he was nervous, but that was the only time I ever saw it happen.

Lyle went into Mom's and pulled out the lavender column dress and blazer she wore every Christmas. It was the one Dad gave her that made her say, "I wish I could wear this every day."

"Where do you think Mom and Dad are right now?" I asked him the next morning after I got back from dropping off the clothes.

He was holding the ladder steady for me as I scraped great handfuls of moldy leaves from the gutters into a trash bag. We talked about the funeral as if we were putting together an event for someone we'd never met. This morning I realized that I didn't know what my brother believed. Was he religious? Did he believe in God? Do I?

"Perkin's Mortuary, 12th and Forest Grove," he said, watching the thick globs of rancid-smelling slop that sloshed over the edge of the drain as they trickled down the ladder's sterling aluminum legs.

"Don't be shitty. You know what I mean."

I tried to catch his eye so I could see what his words meant, if that was all he believed or if he was just sticking it to his big brother like usual. But he wouldn't look up. He kept his gaze fixed on the ladder.

"I don't know," he answered, his voice flat. "Does it matter? We'll all find out someday. No point in thinking about it now."

"Yeah, I guess you're right," I said, turning back to the gutters. "I just wonder sometimes, you know?"

He didn't answer, but I knew it was bothering him. Our parents had been out picking up his medication when that truck slid across thirty feet of black ice to pin them against the brick wall of Peter Johnson's pharmacy. I worried that he blamed himself. I wanted him to know that I didn't, but I couldn't think of a way to bring it up without making things worse.

It didn't seem like there was much point in pushing him. Lyle wouldn't talk unless he was ready, so I went back to the gutters. I used a thick pair of rubber gloves to scrape the rotting leaves down toward the edge of the house, leaning out to scoop the bottom layer that was more slime than leaves. Then the ladder lurched. I grabbed for the gutter, but it broke free from the roof under my weight. I heard a sickening *snap* amidst the clatter of metal, rocks, and leaves. Then my brother shouted something unintelligible. I untangled myself from the ladder's aluminum limbs and scrambled to my feet.

A broken drain pipe had Lyle pinned to the ground with his arm bent at an impossible angle behind his back. It was broken.

I lifted the pipe off him, heaving it aside. It was heavier than it should have been, stuffed full of leaves, mud, and rot.

"Come on," I said, pulling him to his feet. "You need to get that arm looked at. Let's get in the truck. I'll drive you to town."

"Get off of me," he spat, shrugging free from my grip and cradling his injured arm.

"Lyle, we're going to the hospital. This isn't up for debate. You need help."

"I'm fine. Don't touch me."

"Why are you mad at me?" I asked. "You're the one who was supposed to be holding the goddamn ladder!"

"Yeah, and I messed up. I always mess up. What else is new?"

I was so disarmed by his hostility that I didn't know what to do. Lyle's eyes were wide, his mouth stretched into a feral grimace. I tried to help him again, but he pulled away from me. I froze with my hand stretched out like those statues of children reaching for God in front of our parents' church.

Instead, I jammed my hand into my pocket and pulled out my keys, slinging the ring around my finger so that they dangled against my palm.

"I'm going to wait in the truck," I said, trying to keep the hurt from my voice. "Meet me in there when you're done being a stubborn ass. We don't have to talk."

Then I crunched across our parent's lawn to the old Bronco and slammed the door. I didn't have to wait long. Not even two songs went by on the radio before Lyle begrudgingly climbed into the passenger seat. He had trouble pulling himself into the tall truck with only one good arm, but I didn't offer to help. I just watched as he wormed his way into the seat.

We didn't talk on the way there or on the way back. The hospital threw a cast on him and told him to take it easy for a few days. They apologized for not being able to give him pain meds because of his history, but Lyle just shrugged.

"It doesn't hurt that bad," he said. "I'll be fine."

It rained the next day. I gathered up the wet trash bags full of leaves we'd left on the lawn and piled them all into the bin. Fixing the broken gutter would have to wait until the weather cleared up. Instead, I went inside and started pulling the insulation out of the rafters. The pink padding was rotten, chock-full of mold spores and asbestos. This stuff had been up here since the '70s. We used to play cloud pirates in it when we were kids, fighting with plastic swords for mastery over the heavenly seas.

It took a few hours, but I managed to bind the sheets of fluffy pink poison into tight, chorded rolls that I left stacked in the garage. I would have put them out with the trash, but the bins were already full from the leaves and I didn't want the rolls to get sodden with rain.

I'd just unrolled the new baby blue insulation and was using a nail gun to drive it into the wooden beams when Lyle climbed gingerly up into the rafters.

"Why don't you take a break and let me do that for a while?" he asked, holding out his hand for the nail gun.

"Are you crazy? You shouldn't even be up here with that arm."

"Don't worry about it," he said, smiling as he held up his uninjured arm and wriggled around on the beam. He was pinching the wood between his legs to keep himself steady. "Who needs arms when you've got thighs that could flatten a soup can? Give me the nail gun."

He held out his hand for it, but I didn't give it to him.

"I've got this. Why don't you go make us some lunch or something while I finish up here? It shouldn't take long."

"I can do it, Billy," he said. He wasn't smiling anymore.

Could I trust him not to hurt himself? He's been having a lot of accidents lately, but then, what would he do if I don't give it to him?

"If I wanted to hurt myself, I wouldn't need a nail gun," he said, as if reading my mind.

Was I that obvious? I felt ashamed that he knew what I was thinking. All the humor was gone from his voice now. His mossy green eyes were locked onto mine, challenging me to say no.

"Alright, little brother," I sighed, handing over the gun. "I hope you like tuna on white because that's what you get when you make me do the cooking."

I lowered myself to the ground and left him to it. After a few seconds, I heard the dull *thump* of nails driving into wooden beams.

I went into the kitchen to make the sandwiches. I didn't even have to think about which drawer to open to find the can opener or a large bowl. Everything was right where Mom left it. The house was full of our parents in little ways like that. Every room was a needle prodding my heart. Dad's keys were still hanging on the hook by the door, for God's sake. I took a deep breath to steady myself, trying to push back the urge to cry. I had to hold it together. Otherwise, Lyle really would be alone.

I heard the *crack* of the beam splitting before I was done mixing in the mayo.

He wouldn't get out of bed the next day. I thought he was having trouble because of his injuries at first. I wanted to give him his space, but I started to worry as it pushed into the afternoon. My brain wouldn't stop picturing all the terrible things that could be keeping him as the day wore on. I crept up the stairs, careful to step over the squeaky floorboard outside our parent's bedroom. Then I pushed his door open slowly.

"Come to check on me?" he asked, not looking at the door, but staring at a large, black split in the ceiling. It had somehow spidered its way across the entire room, making the walls and ceiling look like fractured glass.

"Well, yeah," I replied. "I was worried about... you know."

"You thought I tried to kill myself again," he said.

His words were harsh, but I could hear the pain underneath them, the guilt. I was right, then. He did blame himself.

The cracks in the drywall started to spread across the ceiling, sprinkling white dust into the carpet.

"It isn't your fault, Lyle," I said, spitting out the words before I had a chance to think about how he'd hear them. I needed to say it. "It could have happened any time. There's nothing anyone could have done."

"It didn't happen any time though, did it?" he asked. "It happened when they were coming to see *me*–because they were worried about *me*."

"Well, now I'm worried about you," I said, trying to regain some control of my voice. "There's no changing the past, little brother. We have to learn to get by with what we have."

"I hate this house," he said, and the roof groaned as if in response to his voice.

He looked at me, his eyes wet with tears. He looked like my little brother again. The one whose hand Mom made me hold whenever we crossed the street; the good-looking boy who girls whispered about even though he was too shy to talk to them. Not the sad twenty-year-old who was found alone in his apartment with a stomach full of painkillers.

Then the ceiling collapsed on him. It buried my brother in an avalanche of wood, tile, and crumbled drywall. I could just see his head, poking out from beneath the rubble as he gasped for air in the plume of white dust.

"Lyle!" I shouted, running over. I grabbed the biggest beam and tried to pull it off him, but it was too heavy. The old, rotten oak wouldn't budge an inch from where it sat, crushing my brother's brittle ribs. It was too heavy.

"Hurry up," I said. "Help me lift it."

"I can't," he groaned, his voice now a thin reed of a whisper.

"Yes, you can," I cried. "We have to get it off you. The whole place is coming down."

"I know. Leave me."

"No."

"Big brother," he whispered. And from somewhere beneath the dust and ruin, his hand shook loose so that he could grab mine. He squeezed it with all the feeble strength he could muster. "Go."

I looked at my little brother. He was the boy I'd once told that eating a glow fly would give him superpowers. I remembered when I first heard him singing and realized he had the voice of an angel, but lacked the confidence to share it. I thought about the time I broke my leg falling out of a blind when we were out hunting with Dad. He carried me back to the lodge even though I must have weighed a good fifty pounds more than him. He was so strong.

"No," I repeated.

And I sat there, holding my brother's hand as ghosts brought the house down on top of him, screaming inside because there was nothing I could do.

How to Look a Wolf in the Eye

Step 1: Never look a wolf in the eye

This will be seen as a challenge and provoke aggression. You might think that by staring into pale yellow retinas, sharpened by millennia of carnivorous instinct, you can display dominance and force the beast to back down. You would be wrong. Wolves are not dogs. They don't have ten thousand years of slavery bred into them.

A wolf would never shirk from a challenging glare, the way you did when your boss asked you to work another weekend. Even though you'd worked the last three. Even though you promised your wife that you would take the kids ice skating. Wolves don't nod in deference, tucking their tails as they resign themselves to Rachael's angry glare, feeling in the pit of your stomach that she's lost that much more respect for you.

Trying to explain would have been useless. She knew how badly you needed your job. She knew that Kevin's orthodontia cost a fortune and that your company's health insurance was the only way you'd be able to afford it. She knew that Lisa's friends all had ten-speed mountain bikes they rode on trails in the Echo Hills every Sunday, and it was eating you up inside that you hadn't been able to get her one. These things made sense, but she still wished you were the kind of man who had control of his life. She wished you could look your boss in the eye and say no. So did you.

This will not work on wolves once they've made it to your door, however. They're animals. They'll rip you to pieces, eviscerate your organs, and eat you from the inside out. They are as wild as the sickness, rampaging through your blood.

Step 2: Don't be afraid

This is the hardest part. Showing fear to a wolf is just as bad as challenging one. This will let the animal know you're its prey. And make no mistake, you *are* prey. Your survival is on the line. Don't convince yourself that you're some kind of hero, that you have control over your fate—that you're anything other than a paper boat being tossed against the rocky Pacific tide.

Remember when you were eleven and your older brother Lewis got sick. That first time you had to pretend that you were brave, even though nightmares woke you in a bitter sweat and you hadn't taken a solid shit in weeks. Remember feeling every muscle in your face, like a web of brittle rubber bands, as you forced a smile while he cracked his jokes, his voice weak and alien. Think about the bloodstains in your pants pocket from where your fingernails bit into your palm when you tried to fight back the chasm that was opening up beneath your feet.

Don't think about how weird it was when you had to start walking to school by yourself, or when your mother tried to give you his clothes. These things are counterproductive.

Practicing this will help you to hide your indomitable well of fear. Wolves can't actually smell it. That's just a myth. They can only smell your sweat, your urine, and the slow drip of cortisol and epinephrine being squeezed out of your adrenal glands to make your heart thump and your brain race.

Take a deep breath. Let it out slow.

Step 3: Make yourself appear scary. Shout, throw stones, and raise your arms over your head

Wolves are apex predators. They won't be deceived into believing that you could possibly pose a serious threat. At best, your thrashing will seem to them like a hissing beetle, warning you not to touch it. They know they can kill you, but if you hiss loud enough—and they aren't too hungry—maybe you can get them to find easier prey.

If it helps, think about your fourteenth summer, when your parents sent you to camp. It was the only time in your life that you tried your hand at pushing people around. You didn't do it on purpose. No one wakes up and thinks, "I'm going to be a bully today."

On the first morning, one of the boys in your cabin was crying because he missed his family. You don't remember his name. You only remember the well of anger that rose inside you. His family didn't go anywhere. They were alive and waiting at home for him. What right did he have to cry? You twisted his arm and told him to knock it off, that his bitching was giving you a migraine. You'd never had a migraine, but your mother got them sometimes and it was what she said whenever you and Lewis were too loud. You knew it was mean and ugly, but you did it anyway. It hurt, but it also felt good, like picking a scab.

No one there knew how weak you were. It was easy to bluster around the camp, acting like pain belonged to you—like it was a knife and you were the surgeon, guiding it into whomever you chose with dexterity and precision. The other kids didn't try to stop you. They should have. You wish they had.

Does that give you confidence? You should be ashamed if it does. The wolves don't care either way. Being a bad person doesn't make your meat taste any different to them. But maybe if your swagger could convince those other kids you were a threat, there might be a chance it will convince the wolves that you aren't worth the effort.

Step 4: Don't turn your back on them

Running from a wolf is just about the worst thing that you can do. Remember that wolves are hunters by nature. They are what is known as *coursing predators*, meaning they take their prey on the run. One will latch its jaw on the tendons at your heel, allowing your own momentum to bring you down. Then another will grab you by the neck and hold you in place for the rest of the pack to eat.

You envy this about the wolves, wishing you'd had this instinct when your father left. You understand why he did it. Life was never the same after Lewis died. Your mother quit her job at the supermarket and spent her days locked in her bedroom with the curtains drawn shut. Loud noises pained her, so you had to learn to be quiet whenever you were home.

You started stealing things when no one was watching you. Just little things, like the change from his dresser or your mother's pain medicine. This was how you found his stash of dirty magazines. It was exciting until you realized these same women had aroused your father and the image sapped any joy out of the experience, so you put them back unused. You wonder if he ever noticed.

Sometimes you picture yourself doing the same thing to your family. You'd tell Rachael that you were going to take a quick trip to the store. Then kiss Kevin and Lisa on the forehead, asking them to be good for their mother, before disappearing from their lives forever. The thought makes you sick. You decide you would never do that, no matter how hard it gets—no matter what your other failings may be.

This makes you feel better. It isn't a high bar, but you'll always be a better father than him. You'll never run.

This may be all that keeps you alive.

Step 5: Curl up into a ball and protect your head, neck, face, and sides

This is a last resort, a Hail Mary, to be used when the above steps have not deterred the wolves and one of them manages to bring you down. The odds of successfully protecting yourself are not high. This is the final flare, arching like a red comet into the night sky from a sinking ship.

It wouldn't be the first time though, would it?

There were always miracles, like when Kevin started coughing blood and Rachael rushed him to the hospital. You left work without a word and slammed your way through traffic, nearly killing a family of four that were crossing the 101. You were sweating through your blazer as your brain struggled to grab onto a single coherent thought, but each was like a hornet in an angry swarm. You tried to reassure your wife, but you kept forgetting to breathe. You remembered Lewis when his skin was stretched so tight around his bones that his knuckles looked like beads on a string. You struggle with the image of the child-sized coffin—wheat wood, because your parents couldn't afford mahogany. It was enough to make you vomit, and you did.

The hospital staff was ready for this. They took you to a room and gave you oxygen while your wife was left to fill out the paperwork. You hated yourself, your weakness, but your body eventually started to relax. You prayed to a god you hadn't thought about in sixteen years. You begged.

A nurse named Amber brought you back to the waiting room when you were calm enough for the hospital staff to trust you again. The doctor came out and told you that your son had Pneumonia. He said that they'd removed the fluid from his lungs and the worst was over. They would have to keep him in the hospital for a while, but Kevin was going to be okay. You hugged your wife and daughter. You shook the doctor's hand, and you thanked the god that you wouldn't think about again until you were surrounded by wolves.

Step 6: Look the wolf in the eye

It could be that none of this will work. There are times when you can't run, or hide, or fight. There are times when doctors use words like "hereditary" and "terminal." When lawyers start asking you how you want to divide your possessions, and you think about which of your things will make your children remember you fondly. What can you give them so that they forgive you for dying? You never really forgave Lewis.

You feel the beasts' hot breath against your neck, the sharp edges of their fore teeth as they pry away your fingers. It's no use telling them you don't want to leave, or that your family needs you. You can't bargain with wolves. You are going to die.

At that moment, all you can do is look the wolf in the eye and meet him.

BLOODLESS

A river stands between us, brother.
  The water passed your lips. You swallowed,
  and now you sleep on distant shores.

  I wear your hand-me-downs, not crying
  to see your ghost in window sills,
  dressed in your old skin. I dream,

  I breathe the void of stolen air,
  while the guard dog holds you in his teeth,
  and I don't know what to do.

PAN'S SHADOW

"Do you remember when we used to watch Peter Pan?" Dante asked the man sitting beside his hospital bed.

"Are you kidding? I couldn't forget if I tried. Your mother pulled us out of school to see it. You were so excited that you forgot to act sick in front of the teacher. She almost didn't let us leave. Your mom had to make up some sort of disease and tell her it was contagious."

"That's right! Then she took us to that old theater attached to the bowling alley. That place was a heap. You could hear the pins crashing on the lanes whenever the movie got quiet. They didn't even have projectors that fit the color reels, so we had to see the movie in black and white. I didn't understand my family's financial situation at the time. I didn't realize that was all we could afford," Dante said. He frowned thoughtfully as he paused to scratch the place on his hand where an IV dripped into his bruised veins. The rough-spun gauze surrounding the needle was blocking him from getting at the source of his irritation, but it felt good to try. "Mom probably had to scrimp for a week just to get those tickets."

"Probably."

"I don't think it mattered, though. I loved that movie. I wanted to move to Neverland, do you remember? I played Peter when we got home and you were my trusty Shadow."

"Of course I do. You jumped off the roof."

Dante started to cough. He reached for the plastic cup on his bedside table and took a small sip of water before continuing. "I was trying to fly. Don't play innocent. You were encouraging me."

"I was not. I was waiting to catch you in case you actually did it."

"But you didn't catch me! I broke my collarbone, my wrist, and two of my fingers. I was in a sling for over a month. It's lucky that bush was there or I might have broken my neck!"

"I would have caught you."

"Maybe. I suppose I can't blame you just because I was an idiot. You didn't make me jump. I wish I could say it was the last time I was so reckless, but we both know that isn't true. That's the funny thing about being young. Nothing scares you more than the idea of people thinking you're afraid."

Dante's eyes drifted for a moment. His memory seemed to work differently than it once had. It was like a tide that pushed and pulled. Sometimes he would struggle to conjure details he knew he should remember, then the tide would come back in and he would almost drown in them. Some of them felt so real that only the pain he felt wracking his withered body kept him grounded in his hospital bed.

"I was thinking about Charlotte the other day," he said.

"The one with the teeth?"

Dante looked incredulous.

"No, Charlotte Baker, the artist, the beautiful one—long brown hair, amber eyes like honey? She was my first love, I think."

"Yeah. She had crooked teeth. You have the memory of a goldfish."

"Keep that lip and we'll see whose teeth are crooked," Dante threatened, feebly shaking a skeletal fist. The friends smiled at each other. "We took that road trip to Crater Lake?"

"And you rode Jose Martinez's dirt bike off the dock. You went under with the bike and then came back up with the big bloody gash on your head. I swam out to get you, but Jose got there first. Good thing too. He knew CPR."

"I was trying to impress a girl." Dante shrugged.

"I'm sure she was swooning. At least you ended up kissing somebody," his friend said, jeeringly. "I would have let you drown if you ruined my bike like that."

Dante let out a weak chuckle and took another sip of water. The tubes and monitors attached to his arms made the task difficult, but the drugs left his mouth so dry that he couldn't go long without a drink.

"I suppose it's all for the best," he said. "If I hadn't embarrassed myself in front of Charlotte, then I might have still been chasing her instead of getting together with Cindy."

"You never told me how you two met."

"No? It's a hell of a story. How have you never heard it?"

"Easy, you never told me."

"Alright, alright. Where to begin?" Dante said, rubbing his hands together. "I'd just moved to Eugene for school. I didn't know my way around yet, so I was looking at a map when I rear-ended this Chevy Impala. I was sweating, believe me. I kept picturing some giant biker-type shoving his way out of the car to come kick my ass. I thought about driving away, but fear kept me frozen to the seat. Then out comes this little redhead."

"Did you think she was going to go easy on you?"

"Maybe for a second. My relief didn't last long, though. She stomped up to my window and started smacking that massive gaudy ring of hers on the glass, telling me to get out of the car. Traffic started piling up behind us while she was letting me know how she felt about my driving, but not a single soul got out and said anything to her. I think everyone else was just as afraid as I was. Then she snatched my insurance information out of my hand and left me standing, shame-faced, in front of a half-mile of bystanders."

"Hell of a first impression."

"It's easy to forget she has that in her. She told me she had older brothers, and I thought maybe that was where she got her temper, but Jack and Terry turned out to be the mellow ones in the family," Dante said. His words occasionally slipped into a dry wheeze. Talking was getting harder for him, but he wanted to keep the conversation going. He wasn't ready to be alone yet.

"Anyway, I nearly turned around and went straight home, but smoke started pouring out of the engine compartment and I was worried my car wouldn't make the trip. So, I went back to my dorm instead. I stayed up half the night worrying what my dad would say when he found out about the car. Then Cindy called. She told me my insurance didn't check out, and she wanted me to meet her at a bar to get it sorted. I was still nursing a few ring-shaped bruises, but I was more scared of what she'd do if I didn't go. She had my address, after all."

"Smart man."

"She looked like something out of a movie when I got there. She was wearing this violet dress with a neckline that went, well, a fair bit below the neck. She bought me a beer and apologized for shouting. I told her I was new in town and she offered to show me around. By the time I realized she wasn't going to ask about my insurance... well, you know."

"That's a good story."

"Christ, how long have we been sitting here?" Dante said, looking out the window and watching as the last crimson spikes of sunlight dissolved into the pale violet evening. "I've been prattling on so long the sun's going down."

"They say you know that you're old when you start spending more time thinking about the past than the future," his friend said. "It's fine though. I don't mind listening."

"I knew I was old before you came around to point it out."

"Well, you don't look it."

"Liar," Dante snorted, adjusting his blanket to keep himself warm. "You know what they don't tell you about chemo? You don't just lose the hair on your head. My legs are balder than your wife's."

"That's not as impressive a statement as you might think."

"Really?" Dante asked, cocking an eyebrow. "My Cindy always kept hers smooth as silk. I remember when she went into labor with Ian. I was running around the house in a panic, trying to gather up all the stuff that I was supposed to have already packed. But while I'm doing that, she goes and draws herself a bath and starts shaving! Can you believe that? She said we'd be watching the video for years and she didn't want to have gorilla legs. I said no one was going to be looking at the stubble on her legs when she was shoving out a person."

"I bet she loved that."

"Gave me the silent treatment right up until the shouting started. I swear, I've never been so terrified in my life. The doctors made me wait outside while I had to listen to Cindy scream her lungs out in an operating room."

"I remember."

"What do you mean, you remember?" Dante asked, "You weren't there."

"Yes, I was."

"You most certainly were not. I've never felt so alone in my entire life as I did sitting in that disease-soaked chair."

"Memory of a goldfish," his friend chided gently. "I was sitting right there next to you the whole time. I brought the cigars, remember?"

"Oh yeah," a slow grin spread across Dante's sore-spotted face. "That nurse looked like she was ready to throttle the life out of us. I was so startled that I dropped mine right in my lap and burned a hole through my jeans. Ended up being checked into the bed right next to Cindy's."

They both laughed for a full minute. Dante kept on chuckling until his chest burned and his throat went raw. It felt good to laugh, even though it hurt. Everything hurt now. There was no point in avoiding it.

His friend was still grinning when Dante's expression went sour. He heaved a deep and sobering breath that went down into his stomach as the tide of memory came back in and he re-lived what happened next.

"And you were there when Ian died too, weren't you?"

The room was quiet.

"You were there when the doctors took him from Cindy's arms and put him in that incubator. When they told us he could still make it—and then he didn't."

His friend opened his mouth to speak, but Dante raised his hand, holding the silence in memory of his lost boy. His tear ducts could no longer adequately lubricate his eyes, so they simply itched and grew red as he shook with the memory.

"He'd be nineteen by now," Dante continued. "He'd be driving. Maybe off at college or maybe back at home crying with his mother about his dying dad. Wouldn't that be something? Maybe he'd have a girl, or a boy, or even a pet dog to help him get through the nights when I'm gone. He'd move on and build a life, but he'd remember me and know that I loved him. I would have liked that."

The silence dissolved slowly, the way pressure builds in your ears with altitude. The only sounds were the robotic beeping of the heart monitor and the metal hinges on the adjustable bed that groaned under the weight of Dante's tremors.

"Do you want me to go?"

"Don't you dare. You keep your ass planted right where it is," Dante replied. His voice was steadier than it had a right to be. "Oh yes. You were there for everything. I remember that now. You were there when Ian died. You were there when Cindy left. You were there when the barrel was in my mouth. You were there when I wanted to go see my son, and you said no."

"That's right, I did," his friend responded.

Dante lurched forward in his bed. The needle in his hand tore free from his tissue-thin skin, causing a crimson stain of blood to blossom through the gauze. The monitor's rhythm picked up to a gallop.

"Why?" Dante challenged.

"You weren't ready."

"But you think I am now?"

"Aren't you?"

Dante stared back into eyes he suddenly felt he didn't recognize. The old man wanted to hit the one he'd always thought of as his friend—his trusted shadow. He wanted to get out of bed, take three swift steps across the room and thump him right in the teeth. It would probably kill him to do it, but oh, it would feel good.

Then, seemingly out of nowhere, a smile bloomed across Dante's face as the answer to what his friend meant dawned on him.

"Cindy." Dante said the name softly. "Did you send her?"

"I don't have any idea what you're talking about. Did Cindy come to see you?" his friend replied. He was the picture of innocence but for the smile tugging at the corner of his mouth. "It's about time. You're not getting any younger."

"She came by during visiting hours this afternoon. She told me it wasn't my fault."

"Did you believe her?"

"You know what? I think I did."

Dante's friend got out of his chair and walked over to the side of the bed. The gloom slipped away and Dante could see him clearly for the first time. His silhouette was tall and graceful. He was dressed in simple clothes that were black as shadow, nearly obfuscating the slender, charcoal-feathered wings tucked gracefully behind his shoulders. Dante gazed into eyes that looked like galaxies—eyes that had seen the beginning and end of all things, but were watching him now with kindness.

"So now you're ready," he said. "That's good, because it's time for us to go."

The heart monitor's beeping turned to an annoyingly constant note, so Dante's friend disconnected the leads from his chest. Dante's friend slid his arms under the old man's shriveled body and lifted him out of the sheets. His skin had gone cold, but that was fine. He was about to go somewhere warm. It amazed Dante to find that the transition didn't hurt at all. His shadow had finally caught him, the way he'd promised back when Dante first tried to fly, and all the pain slipped away.

"Where are we going?" he asked.

"Second star to the right and straight on till morning," his friend answered.

A DRAFT FOR REJECTION

The sting of rejection bears a venom like no other. It courses deep into your heart and nestles there, like a worm, wriggling against your pride. This draft will be a balm for your heart, an antidote for the worm, and a fire that shall scorch the very souls of your enemies. To begin, you will need a cauldron, a flame, and a large wooden spoon.

Set the flame to roughly the temperature of hell. It should be a blazing inferno that would boil the sea and send the armies of man scurrying in pain and fear as blisters bubble beneath their tender flesh. Ash wood works nicely, but birch will do in a pinch. Also, remember to check that your cauldron is thoroughly clean. Any impurities could inadvertently lead to the extinction of a small, land-based animal. (Remember the Dodo!)

Once you have your tools prepped, you can begin.

We will begin by using water from the river Styx as the base of our broth. I know it's pricey, but you won't be doing yourself any favors in trying to save a penny by buying Nile water. Let us not forget that Achilles would have been truly immortal if only his mother had the foresight to double dip. You will need those protective qualities to shield your heart from the slings and arrows of those who haunt you—those who cut you where no ointment or bandage could reach.

Next, you will need to season the broth. For the best effect, I recommend salt harvested from the tears of a martyr. It doesn't have to be Galileo or Joan of Arc, but it must be a genuine martyr.

Be cautious! False martyrs are much more common than the genuine article and their tears will do nothing but sour the brew with self-pity. Real martyrs hold fast to their beliefs even unto their deaths. This will erase the self-doubt that has been whispering in your ear like that old trickster serpent. It will reassure you of the true path and the rightness of those who follow it. You may also add lavender for a more soothing and pleasant aroma.

After that, you will add three raven tongues for their ability to capture human speech. You might be wondering, "Why not parrot?" Well, parrot tongues certainly have their uses. They're a bit like the cayenne pepper of witchcraft, exotic and a little spicy. A parrot's tongue might do if you're simply seeking to make your enemies uncomfortable. Perhaps you'd like them to be attacked by a swarm of bees, or have them be chosen for a random audit come tax season, but nothing beats raven tongue if you seek to rend your enemies to their very souls. Their astral forms shall come limping to the gates of hell where the great Beelzebub will struggle to find a torment vile enough to match the one you yourself have cast upon them. Do not spare the rod. You bore your soul to these mongrels and they spat on it. I can think of no reason why you should be so gentle with theirs.

Now for the vegetables!

Leeks are always nice. Garlic is good for the blood and adds a lot of flavor. Potatoes are fine if you're looking to make it heartier but remember, you will have to add more martyr tears to compensate for the extra starch. I've found that you can add carrots to just about anything, but clover is the real secret. Not only does it add nutrients without compromising the flavor, but it will also bring you luck.

And you're going to need luck. Because eventually, you will open your heart again. It might not feel like it while the blood organ is wounded so painfully and so deep, but the injury will close in time and you'll see that there are others who are more worthy of your trust. There are those whom you will care for with such passion and such completeness of your being that you will not be able to abide that thin layer of membrane which divides. You will tear your own heart open to let them in.

You will do this because you are strong.

Lower heat, let simmer for six days, six hours, and six minutes, then serve under the light of a new moon.

4:23 AM

Boiling, boiling, boiling, boiling.
   Skin creeping, itching, crawling.
   Feels like crying, struggling, dying.

   Awake. Painfully awake.

   Feels like more than I can take.
   Fuzzy brain, no focus. Pain.
   Feet leap, tick, creep.
   Itches deep, no sleep, no sleep.

   Close my eyes. Clamp them tight.
   Whole body tight, tight, tight.
   Wrung, and sprung, and full of flight.
   Please, God, let me sleep tonight.

BENEATH THE ICE

My dad used to take me ice fishing before he got hurt. Sometimes he'd open the door to my bedroom when the morning was still dark and shake me awake. He'd whisper for me to put on my parka, telling me that I wasn't going to school today as I blinked the sleep from my eyes and tried to find his silhouette against the black pre-dawn. I never knew when he was going to do it. He never gave any hints or secret signals the night before. Sometimes I wondered if Mom even knew. Was there some unspoken understanding between them that there would occasionally be mornings when she would wake up to find her husband and daughter gone?

He'd crank up the volume on his truck's stereo once we were out of earshot from the little town and we'd listen to the stash of old rock cassette tapes he kept tucked in a cardboard box under his seat. The speakers were slightly blown-out, but we still sang along to *Let it Bleed* and *Exile on Main St.* We'd belt out the half-remembered lyrics until we arrived at the collage of brightly colored shacks nestled on the frozen Hudson Bay.

Now I was making the trip by myself. I was worried that the old clunker wouldn't start as I turned the key in the ignition, but it immediately greeted me with the warm rumble of firing cylinders. The stash of tapes was right where he left them, too. I decided to make the drive out of Churchill in silence this time, though. It didn't seem fun to sing on my own.

I felt the icy top layer of snow break under my boots when I got out of the truck near the bay. The frost gave every step a sense of crunchy satisfaction, something I'd missed while I was away at school. The ice was perfectly flat out here. It was a placid sea of glittering white that stretched into the dark horizon.

The town of Churchill, Manitoba was located beside a special nook in the Hudson. A unique gyre in the current kept the water here from being swept away, making it the first part of the bay to freeze in the winter. Tourists came during these early frosts to see the polar bears hunting on the ice. I usually tried to give both the tourists and the bears their space.

There'd been snow in Toronto too, but it was dirty and rough. Even after a fresh fall, you could see the curve of the street sleuthing toward the drain, the sharp rises of sidewalk, and the lumps of buried cars. They gave the white blanket an uneven keel.

I pulled the drill from the truck bed. It cut a swath through the fresh powder like a knife scraping through frosting as I dragged it to my father's fishing shack. The inside was smaller than I remembered. It'd always been a tight fit for Dad and me, but I thought that was because he was so big. The bulkiness of his grandfather's old caribou parka puffed him up till he filled half the tiny steel box. Now I fit inside easily, but it was still uncomfortable, like sitting in a cupboard with the shelves pressing in.

The floor latch stuck when I first tried to open it. I pulled a can of WD-40 out of Dad's bag. But as I was pulling it out, the sound of tiny pebbles tumbling against hard plastic came from the side pocket.

I froze with the metal can clutched like a grenade in my hand. I felt my saliva glands gush at the sound.

What was I doing pretending I cared about fishing, anyway? Why didn't I just drop the pretense, take out the bottle I'd buried in there, and do the thing I really came here for? Pressure was building in the peak of my spine, threatening to send its tendrils worming into my brain.

Not yet.

I sprayed a wet layer of metallic-smelling grease onto the latch's seams. Then I turned to the little generator, filling its tank with fresh gas and plugging in the rusted iron radiator. It was too loud to run when the lines were in the water, but Dad insulated the shack so it would hold the heat for a few hours.

He never needed the radiator. The cold didn't bother him. He only ever turned it on for me. The ancient rig still functioned perfectly though, giving off waves of dry, prickly heat that quickly filled the little shack.

I gave the latch another tug. It groaned a weak protest but gave way to the lubrication that'd soaked into its swollen seams. The steel door creaked up into the cabin and revealed the ice underneath. Now the hatch was open, I brought out the drill and plugged it into the genny too.

Drilling the fishing hole was messy work. The machine churned the glassy ground into a wet slush that would shoot everywhere if you weren't careful. I slipped up a couple of times, sending a few chips of ice flying into the radiator to sizzle and spit, but it wasn't long before I felt a *plop* as the bit punched through to the water below.

It was strange looking down at the inky gray surface of the Hudson. It felt exactly like it did when I was little. That sudden realization that there was a whole world of water under my feet, picturing all the different kinds of colossal creatures that could be lurking down there without my ever knowing it.

I put the drill away and turned off the generator. Without the soft puttering of the little engine, the shack was quiet enough that I could hear the wind hissing around the walls and the gentle slap of the current against the frozen ground.

That silence was always a little unnerving. I remember asking Dad if we could play music in here like we did in the truck.

"Not if you want to catch anything," he whispered in response. "The water is like a giant ear to the fish. You have to be very quiet if you want them to relax enough to take a nibble."

Instead, he whispered stories to me. They were fables he'd heard from the Paallirmiut. He had friends in the tribes and sometimes visited them when taking supplies north to Arviat. He told me about the abused, blind boy named Lumiuk, who found his sight in the sea, and the goddess Sedna, who was cast into the ocean where she became the keeper of all the seals, dolphins, and whales.

I liked these stories, but Dad knew that the scary ones were my favorite. I was addicted to that hair-raising chill that had nothing to do with the cold. So, he would recite them to me on those dark mornings when the shack was silent except for water licking against the ice. He'd tell me about the sinewy blue demon Mahaha who giggled as he prowled the Arctic, barefoot, but unbothered by the sleet and snow. How he searched for travelers to tickle to death with his delicate fingers, leaving their corpses with a twisted, frozen smile. He'd tell me about the shadow people who whisper but are never seen, and the shapeshifters that can look like any animal but can't hide their burning red eyes. There were the giant Inupasugjuk and the barbaric Tuniit. But to me, the most terrifying creatures were the Qallupilluk. They were scaly fish-people who lived under the ice, humming as they dragged children into the water, never to be seen again. They reeked of sulfur and wore traditional amauti made from eider duck, like the ones Inuit women once used to carry their babies.

I listened as he whispered their stories, and wondered why they took the children. No one knew. Their motivations weren't part of the fable. Did they simply like the way children tasted, or were they lonely creatures, longing for companionship? I wondered if they were the souls of mothers who'd lost children, aching to fill the holes in their hearts.

I thought about these stories as I sat on the little wooden bench at the far end of the shack. I baited the line and fed it into the water. Then I watched the hook drift slowly out of sight before grabbing a can of beer from Dad's duffel and cracking it open. It was almost too cold, making me hiccup after the first sip. The shack was quiet and uncomfortable, but it was better than spending the day at home.

I was in my apartment when I heard about my dad's accident. I'd been sleeping through a Biology lecture I was too high to attend. I woke up to the sound of my phone buzzing like a hive of angry hornets against my glass nightstand. I ignored the first call, pressing my pillow firmly over my ear, but it wouldn't stop. I knew something was wrong by the third time it went off. I rolled upright, trying to force my blurry eyes to focus on the screen in my hand. The caller ID read, "Home."

"Hello?" I answered, trying my best to sound alert.

There wasn't an answer right away, but I heard the familiar throaty wheezing of my mother on the other end.

"Mama? What's wrong?" I asked.

"It's your dad, Jess," she said, finally managing to force the words through her thick, mucusy sobs. "There was an accident. He fell. We need you to come home."

"Is he okay?" I asked. "What happened?"

She cried in response. I tried to wait for her to choke out the words, but her desperate moans hung in the static between the phones. They were like phantoms of all the horrible things that could have happened. I pictured him tumbling off a roof onto a sharp fence post, tripping down a flight of stairs and breaking his neck against a wall, or falling through the thin ice he'd always been so careful to avoid and drowning in the water he spent his whole life walking over.

I gagged.

Eventually, my mom finally managed to explain what happened. Dad was installing a de-icing cable on the roof when the ladder slipped. He didn't land on a fence post as I'd imagined, but he did shatter three columns of his spine and severely damaged the lower half of his nervous system. She said the doctors hoped he would walk again, but they weren't sure.

I jumped on the first bus home. I worried about my father, and I spent much of the long ride north picturing myself taking care of him, bringing food and medicine to his bedside. An accident like this was terrible, but at least they had me. How many daughters would leave in the middle of a sixteen-unit term, casting aside months of work to take care of their injured father? Maybe it was a selfish thing to want, but I thought they would recognize the sacrifice that I was making for them.

But the reality of my father's pain was more than I imagined. I hadn't realized the nightmare of iron frames and steel pins that held my dad together. The bedpans and catheters which required constant changing, or the screaming in the middle of the night as doctors struggled to balance his pain meds.

I didn't realize how angry he would be all the time either. I could only remember him being angry twice when I was little. The first time was when a trader from Montreal allowed a hundred pounds of caribou meat to rot because he thought the chill of early spring would be enough to preserve it, and the second was when he caught me smoking with my friend Michelle. Now a pot of cold tea could spin him into a rage that took hours to burn off.

I didn't think about how my mother would cry over bills because she'd never had to imagine a world where dad wouldn't be able to work, or how mercilessly desolate it would be to live in a house where no one ever smiled.

But the worst part was the lack of privacy. I hadn't had a moment alone in over a week and my headaches were getting bad.

The fishing line bounced a bit, jarring me out of my bitter reverie. I watched it for a long moment, ready to grab the rod if something had taken the bait, but then it went back to drifting loosely in the icy portal like a hair of crooked light passing through a mirror. The water seemed to vibrate.

Unable to hold out any longer, I reached into the old duffel and pulled out the orange plastic pill bottle I'd hidden in the side pocket. My dad's name was scrolled under the word "Oxycodone." It was just one of the dozen or so half-full bottles of prescriptions of drugs that failed to help control my father's pain. They were scattered around the house the way other families display trinkets from trips they've taken.

My hand shook a little as I held the bottle, making the pills rattle like the tail of a venomous snake.

I'd never done drugs before moving to the city. I didn't even really do them when I got there. I don't have a dramatic story about getting addicted after being pressured at a party or dating some edgy boy with tattoos.

The truth is that I had my wisdom teeth out about six months ago. The procedure went a bit wrong when one of them broke and the surgeon had to cut deep into the gums to get out all the pieces. She gave me twenty pills to cover my recovery. I only needed about half of them before my jaw was pretty much healed, but then finals came and I started getting these really bad headaches.

I tried all the pills you could buy at the student center. I searched the Internet for natural remedies and exercises, but there was only one medicine that helped. I bummed a few oxys off a friend who'd hurt her leg a while back when mine ran out.

Then I met a guy named Pete whose dad was an M.D. He stole one of his father's prescription pads and would write anything you wanted on one for fifty dollars. There was a rumor that he had other methods of collecting payment from girls who were low on cash, but I hadn't had to resort to that yet.

"You a cop?" he asked the first time I approached him.

"How many nineteen-year-old cops have you met?"

"You never know," he said smiling. "Could be older than you look."

His eyes dipped as he looked me up and down, considering me like a lazy cat who was deciding whether or not a mouse is worth climbing out of bed for.

"You have money?" he asked.

My hands shook as I pulled three crumpled twenties out of my pocket.

He folded my change into the script and passed it to me, his eyes searching the room like we were in a spy movie and he was my secret contact. His finger stroked mine as he parted with the paper.

"You didn't get this from me, you understand?" he asked, rattling off the cliché with enough confidence that I was sure he'd said it to other girls.

"I don't even know who you are."

I tried to pretend that I didn't understand what I was getting into with the pills, but the pharmacists didn't make it easy. Every time I tried to exchange one of Pete's scripts, they'd take a break from all their counting and weighing to come to the counter and make sure I know how addictive they were. They gave me pamphlets on opioid addiction with every bottle and stapled them to the instructions for use.

I knew what they were. I knew what I was.

My hand started to shake harder as I gripped the bottle. I almost couldn't make out the drug's four-syllable name through the blurriness that was forming around the edge of my vision.

Then I heard a strange humming. I wasn't sure if the sound was real, or if it was a product of the thick spikes of pain shooting into my skull. I took a deep breath and tried to steady myself.

I would take one. Just one. The pain was too much otherwise. I wouldn't even be able to drive home. Besides, I needed it to go back and face my parents. The idea of doing it straight was too much to bear.

I just needed one now, and maybe a few more to get through his recovery. Then I'd be back in school and I'd never touch them again.

I pressed in the child-locked cap, gently unscrewing it. Four of the tiny pills slid easily into my hand. It was like they were eager to be free of the plastic bottle; like they couldn't imagine anything more comfortable than the plush skin of my palm. I pushed three of them back, leaving one lucky tablet nuzzled into the fleshy crease of my cupped hand.

The humming was getting louder. It grew till the walls vibrated with it. I realized there was a rhythm to the sound. Not a song or even a melody, but a beat that burrowed into my chest. It filled me so completely that I worried my heart would stop without it, and it would leave me empty.

I looked at the pill. I looked at the portal. A pair of black eyes looked back. The humming stopped.

It took me a minute to register what I was seeing. The sloping brow that curved away from the creature's eyes was patterned with maroon scales. An acid orange pectoral fin lined its back like the stripped skeleton of an ornamental Chinese fan, its barbs tipped with needle-sharp points. A single arm stretched out of the water, webbed like a frog and covered in poisonously bright red bumps. It clung to the lip of the portal, securing itself within the warmth of the shack. There was a smell too, like rotten eggs.

The door was on the other side of the hole. I would have to step over the creature to escape. My gut lurched into my ribs as I watched the monster pull itself from the ice, dragging its body over the jagged lip made by my drill and into the ever-closing space between us.

I pulled my legs up onto the bench, looking frantically around the shed for something to defend myself with. I didn't see anything, so I threw the empty beer can.

It glanced off the shoulder of the creature, failing to damage it, but making it snarl in anger. It revealed a wide mouth that was full of narrow, pointed teeth.

It grabbed my ankle and pulled me toward the water. I clung desperately to the bench and filled the Arctic with my screams, even though I knew there wasn't another soul for miles. The creature's muscular fingers squeezed my ankle till it felt like my foot was trapped in an iron vise.

I thrashed and pulled, hurting myself more than the creature, as I bashed my body against the steel walls and shelves. I was trapped. The pain in my head was blinding as pure, adrenalin-soaked panic overrode all rational thought. Two thoughts looped over and over. It's going to kill me. I'm going to die.

More eyes appeared in the water. They were black, lifeless, and as hungry as their sister's. There was no love or pity in them. They were voids of endless, painful want.

Something broke in me, and the animal flight instinct that was coursing through my body suddenly shifted gears. I lifted the foot that had been anchoring me to the wooden bench. With all of my strength, I drove the heel of my three-and-a-half pound, hard, rubber-soled boot into the creature's face.

It looked confused, frowning like it couldn't understand what just happened. Its grip loosened on my ankle, but I couldn't pull free just yet. So, I kicked again and again, beating the creature back to its world beneath the waves.

The open pill bottle that was still in my hand dipped as I continued to drive my foot down and the pearly white tablets plopped gently into the water around her.

As soon as the monster's face was completely submerged, I slammed the hatch closed, turning it tight before racing out of the shack and back to Dad's old truck.

I cranked the ignition and sped off, not stopping until I was safely parked outside the house where my parents raised me. The sun had only just finished making its ascent over the horizon. Most people were just starting to get out of bed. My heart was still hammering in my chest as I slid the keys out of the cylinder, my hands shaking worse than ever. I cried in the cab for a long while, letting the tears and snot roll into my lap without trying to stop them.

I almost died. That could have been it.

I thought about my parents. They were already on the verge of collapse because of Dad's accident. Not knowing why their daughter never came home... It seemed too cruel to even imagine. I also thought about my degree and realized with dry amusement that I would be really upset if I died before I finished it. I wanted my dad to see me graduate, whether he was standing or not.

I wondered if anyone would believe me, or if I should even tell my dad that I finally saw the Qallupilluk he'd warned me about since I was little.

I knew things wouldn't get any easier when I walked back into the house. Dad would still be angry. Mom would still be miserable. Drugs would still be scattered around the house like peppermints. But it was better than the numb, cold I'd just left behind, and now I knew I was strong enough to face it.

FAMILY RECIPE

Winter is here. Bleak gray skies have blanketed the sun's warmth and the rotting autumn has been buried under a layer of crisp, white snow. It's the time of year when you rush home after work, buried in thick coats and scarves, eagerly seeking remedies of warmth and comfort to fight the deep chill—and nothing combats the bitter cold of winter like a warm bowl of Russian cabbage soup.

There are several different kinds of shchi. A sour version of the soup called kislye shchi can be made using sauerkraut, while variations that use sorrel, spinach, and other leafy vegetables are known as green shchi or zelyoniye shchi. Both are delicious, but this recipe is for traditional shchi, which is always made using fresh cabbage.

It's been in my family for generations, going all the way back to my great, great grandmother who lived in the northern country, near Yakutsk, before the revolution. The Russian government has changed twice since she first filled her house with the scent of simmering vegetables, herbs, and hearty stock, but this recipe has stayed the same. She taught it to her daughter, who taught it to my babushka, who finally taught it to my mother after the two of them immigrated to the States when she was a little girl.

Just as I fill the pot with ingredients, this soup fills me with memories of the women in my family. I remember my mother stirring as she danced to the Ramones on the radio, her auburn brown locks pulled back with a length of twine because she always lost her hair ties. My father's face would always light up when he walked through the door. The warm scent of salt and chicken fat melted away the weariness from his long days at the Fulton cannery.

He would come into the kitchen and wrap his arms around her waist from behind. She would pretend to be surprised as she felt his lips peck gently against her neck, eliciting a quiet "oh," as if she hadn't noticed the scent of fish coming off him in waves. Perhaps one of these moments is when I first realized what love looks like.

Sometimes I remember my babushka muttering to herself in Russian while she stirred the pot, her cigarette bobbing in her mouth as smoke curled off the glowing ember to mingle with the steam while ash drifted softly to the tile floor. I was nervous when my parents left me alone with her at first. I wasn't used to the coarse way she cared for me.

One time I stayed home with a cold while my parents were away at work. My aching nose and raw throat were the worst ailments anyone ever had to endure, as far as I was concerned. Baba told me I had too much sympathy for myself, recounting how many of her mother's friends had died when illness had spread to their lungs. She told me about how my great-grandmother took her to visit their graves and told her their stories.

Great-grandma told her that her friend Inessa had golden hair, but that it was always dirty, so most people never knew how beautiful she was. She'd been very good at wrestling stubborn pigs back into their pens and was the best one to go to if ever you had a secret. Baba said it was the only time she'd ever seen her mother cry.

Her face turned strangely solid after that, in the way old faces sometimes do. But I still remember the soothing feeling of the soup sliding down my throat; strips of slick cabbage and lumps of starchy potato filling my stomach and making me feel stronger.

She drew us a warm bath after that. I remember seeing her scars as she lowered herself into the tub. I asked her where they came from and she told me that my grandfather had not been a gentle man, and that was, perhaps, why he drowned.

I didn't understand, but I was afraid to ask.

At times, something strange happens when I eat this soup though. I remember more than just my mother and my babushka. I sometimes remember things that I couldn't have seen—impossible things.

Once, while I was lying in bed and my babushka was tucking me in, I told her about one of the strange memories that bubbled into my mind. She stared at me in wide-eyed horror as I described the old man with paper-white skin. I described his thin, black hair and tangled beard, his wet flesh and eyes that seemed to glow an almost phosphorescent blue. I could picture him clear as day, but I couldn't remember when I'd met him.

I told her about the cottage where I saw the man. It had herbs hanging from the ceiling to dry and old wooden floorboards that were not quite flush so that they creaked when you stepped on them. There was a hearth that was caked in soot, but filled with a warm fire that fought the icy wind which would sometimes whistle through tiny gaps in the walls. It was adorned with kettles and pots and had an oven full of the scent of baking bread.

The old man was dressed in ratty cloth. It was patched, damp, and stained with algae from the river. I remembered watching him take the hand of a beautiful young woman and speak to her in Russian. Perhaps the strangest part was that I understood him perfectly even though I had never learned more than a few words of the language.

"Your mother is gone," he said to the woman in a throaty croak. "But I am not. Do not fret. I will take care of my family."

Although he was dressed like a vagrant, the woman treated him as if he were the Tsar. She bowed her head and kissed his hands, seating him in the only chair that didn't wobble and offering him the last of our honey bread.

"Thank you, Lord Vodník," she said.

And then he smiled. His mouth split wide, like a frog's, revealing toothless gums that stretched from ear to ear. It was a horrifying sight, but the beautiful woman smiled back. Then he removed a porcelain teapot from beneath his robes and set it on the table.

"For you, my child," he said, and then he opened the pot.

I couldn't see what was inside because I was low to the ground, like a toddler, but I glimpsed the intricate design on its side. It had the image of a green-skinned man smoking a pipe as he floated on a log drifting down the river. The woman's expression lit up at the contents of the pot, her beauty cast in an eerie golden glow.

"It is a good one," he said. "It has strength that, I think, will be a great help for you and the little one. I found its former owner trying to build a dam on my river, just above the southern bend."

Then the old man took the teapot and poured it into the cast iron cauldron that was bubbling above the fire, mixing whatever was inside with the simmering vegetables and hearty stock.

"Eat and be well," he said, tucking the teapot back beneath his coat. Then he turned just as he was about to step out the door, his grin shrinking back to a normal human mouth. "And call, should you have need."

I'd never seen my babushka frightened before. The loose skin around her jaw started to quiver as I finished telling the story. Her gnarled hands crushed her cigarette as she balled them into fists.

"That was my memory. Not yours," she whispered. "I was the baby on the floor. The cottage you described is where I was born. It was my mother whom the vodyanoy came to call. I thought I'd imagined him."

"What is he?" I asked.

"Very far away," she said, but something in her voice didn't sound so sure. She paused for a long time. "He is one of the old kind. Very old. He lived in the river near our village. Sometimes he would drown people, and sometimes he would answer our prayers. When I was a little girl, *my* babushka once told me that she wished to the vodyanoy for a child, but many women wished for this, so I thought nothing of it. My mother turned out very beautiful though, and so many people said she was a rusalka. She was always just Mama to me, but perhaps..."

Her voice was feverish at first, but she trailed off at the end. "It is late for this," she said after a long pause. "Go to sleep, little one."

She refused to talk about the old man after that, except to make me promise that I would never tell my mother—*never tell anyone*—that story again. I was a child, and so I promised, not knowing how hard that secret would be to keep once she was gone.

Sometimes I wake up cold in the night and I hear the low croak of his breath. I smell the musk of algae, mingling with cookfire smoke. Then a damp chill sweeps through my apartment. I feel the ache of loss for my babushka who passed this last year, quietly in her sleep, and hear the call of the Hudson rushing toward the sea.

Then I think of another river. One that winds through snow-laden spruce trees and powdered plains. Past animals with thick fur, and hills of sheer rock. A river I've never seen, whose current slides lazily beneath a deceitfully thin sheet of ice. Sometimes, this simple cabbage soup makes me feel closer to that distant place. Sometimes it makes me feel closer to that strange man, but it's the only thing that makes me feel better.

Ingredients:

- 3 tablespoons butter

- 1 large onion, chopped

- 1 large head of cabbage, shredded

- 2 large carrots, peeled and thinly sliced

- 1 stalk celery, chopped

- 8 cups chicken stock

- 2 large russet potatoes, peeled and chopped

- 2 large tomatoes, peeled, seeded, and chopped

- 1 bay leaf

- 1 sprig fresh dill

- Salt and pepper to taste

Instructions:

Melt butter in the bottom of the pot and sauté vegetables at medium-low heat until they are soft. Then add stock and raise the temperature to high, stirring regularly until it reaches a boil. Add bay leaf and lower the temperature, allowing the soup to simmer for an hour. Salt and pepper to taste, garnish with dill, then serve to those you love.

Follow my blog for more recipes.

A STROKE OF FATE

The cabin was small, but that's why I chose it. The bare oak walls and plastic-lined tile floor offered little in the way of distraction. Only the scent of burning metal radiating from the space heater gave the slightest bit of stimulation.

A table sat beside my easel. Brushes, acrylics, towels, water, food, and anything else I might need lay scattered across its stained surface. A blank 28"x36" stretch of bleached canvas stared at me from the shelf. An itch nagged at the callous on my middle finger where the brush would rest. I couldn't wait any longer.

My hands lurched for the mason jar crammed with a bouquet of brushes and came back with a #10 crimped. Bold strokes of crimson would form the base with a blend of something dark for the sake of texture. I'd been scared to put brush to canvas since I was injured, but I knew that there'd be no going back once that first thick layer of red streaked the virgin cloth.

The accident wasn't my fault. You were the one who first taught me to appreciate the elegant botanical aroma in a good gin. You were also the one who insisted on buying those cone-shaped paper cups that we couldn't set down until they were empty. We both had a few drinks—maybe more than we should have—but I don't think I could have seen that truck sliding across the ice on my driest day. Nothing is your fault when you drink, right?

Didn't you blame the wine when we spent three hours chatting in the parking lot after my exhibit? Did the feeling of martinis still saturating your blood help to absolve your guilt when you went home to your husband that first night, knowing that your lips had been pressed against mine just hours before?

I remembered the way things seemed to slow down in the seconds before we collided, the crunch of the roof caving in as I threw my hands over your head. Could I have done more? The pain was easy enough to forget, terrible as it had been, but nothing could make me forget the feeling of your life being smothered between my palms.

Shapes were becoming clear on the canvas. I thought this would be a labor of hours, but whatever devil possessed my hands gifted them with a malevolent dexterity. I wondered for a moment if you were guiding these violent brush strokes, but no. Your touch had been forceful at times, but it was never coarse. The only thing that could break my fervor was the sound of your voice.

Our last argument had soaked into the cabin walls like rot, the soft vibrations of your words permanently absorbed into the fibers. I could still hear them resonating in the grain, like the ocean in a conch shell.

"He knows what we've done so we can't see each other anymore," you said. "Stay away from me. We can't be friends."

I wondered if that was all we'd been. I was certain that we were more than friends, though perhaps less than lovers. Whatever we weren't, I knew that we were important.

It might have simply been my stained hands that enchanted you at first. Maybe the rows of paintings in the gallery marked with my name made you euphoric, but you eventually came to care about me just as I came to care about you.

I memorized your details. I knew the way you smiled wider when you laughed, the intermittent snores and coos as you slept, and the scent of your shampoo. I knew that your sister never forgave you for being your parents' favorite, that the freckles on your shoulder looked like the little dipper, and that you were rusty at the oboe, but could still play "I Got You Babe" in a pinch.

The last strokes of the brush fell like shattered glass. It was almost a portrait of you, except no one was there. The negative space around you was wild with color; a storm of orange, yellow, red, gray, and moonless midnight. You are in the center, and yet you are not. Your skin is emptiness, your eyes a void, your smile a hungry maw.

Then there was light. Not the warm yellow glow of my studio, but a pair of blinding white halogens. I heard the heavy thunder of rain, the garbled sound of Bad Religion playing on the radio, and the blaring of a horn before the high-pitched screech that could only be made when three tons of steel skids like a stone across icy asphalt.

I opened my eyes to the light of the hospital. Florescent bulbs shone like angry stars. To my right was a clear plastic bag labeled "Dilaudid." Its contents were the real artist responsible for that painting–that room.

"Nurse!" I cried; my voice harsh from the night terrors.

The muffled sound of orthotic footsteps preceded a dark-haired woman with bags under her eyes.

"What is it?"

She asked the question pleasantly enough, though I could hear the exhaustion in her voice and the suppressed annoyance that I didn't use the buzzer. If only I could.

"May I have some water?"

She took the glass from my bedside table and held the button to lift me upright. Then I aimed my useless hands—crushed, missing fingers, and full of steel pins—at the plastic bag.

"Can I have some more of that, too?"

"Not for another hour," she said, her voice stern. "I'll come back then."

"Thank you," I replied, trying my best to sound grateful.

I looked at the wreckage that used to be my hands. The doctor said that I would regain some of my motor functions. I would someday be able to hold my own cup and wipe my own ass. I would never be able to shape the delicate lashes of an eye or keep the narrow tendrils of a shadow straight, but I would paint again. It didn't matter that I would never again see my work in a gallery or my name in the headlines. I didn't care. There was only one thing that mattered. That canvas would not be my last.

THE TROUBLE WITH STRAWBERRIES

My favorite fruit is a strawberry.

    Luxurious, ethereal, judiciously tender.

    I could eat them every day,

    for every meal, on every hour, in every single mouthful.

    The taste is sublime—the texture, tantalizing.

    A delicacy made for gods, the ambrosia of hors d'oeuvres.

But there is a problem.

You can't

eat

the seeds.

They hatch, you know?

Like spiders in spring.

Chitinous shell cracks into a nest of pulp,

slender legs, vying for release,

eager to sink their parasitic hooks into soft, subcutaneous tissue,

eager to burrow into fat, and flesh, and vulnerable intestine.

Digging, nesting, injecting their brood.

I hate them.

Hours I've spent, picking them with a needle,
rooting out the invasive aggressors,
and plying them from heaven's fruit.
Plucking, pulling, scooping, and scraping.

You have to be careful. You have to be certain.
You must be sure you got them all.
One is all it takes. One is all they need,
before you are infected, infested, impregnated with them,
and then it's too late...

Blueberries are easier.

DREAM CATCHER

I wasn't blessed by a Navajo medicine man, or crafted from the tanned sinew of a grizzled bison. An old hippie named Georgette made me out of a metal hoop and waxed twine she bought at the local Hobby Lobby. My materials are not sacred, but my purpose remains the same.

Georgette sold me out of the back of her van to a woman named Clementine at a Steve Miller concert. After the transaction was complete, my new owner threw me unceremoniously into the trunk of her car and swiftly forgot I existed. I spent what felt like months buried under reusable grocery bags and an old bathing suit that smelled faintly of mildew. I can't say exactly how much time passed in that darkness, though. It was like the sensation of being trapped between sleeping and waking, where each second seems to stretch forever. I thought the long dark would eventually drive me to madness, but then I met Julian.

It was his birthday when Clementine finally fished me out of the trunk of her car. Her sister was having some trouble with her marriage, and Clementine came to support her. She hadn't remembered that it was her nephew's birthday until after she arrived and discovered a party in full swing.

It disappointed him to peel away the sports section of the local tabloid she'd used as wrapping paper, only to find me concealed within. Yet, his mother made him thank his aunt. Then she hung me above his window so I might serve as a filter for his dreams.

He sees in colors that don't exist. Blues and greens shift into amorphous shades that he won't remember in the morning. They come like shadows on a foggy lens, drifting uncertainly.

Sometimes he tries to make them into something tangible. Something with a name to weigh them down so he can have power over them, like constellations or clouds.

"That one looks like an umbrella," he thinks.

But as if to defy his attempts to force sense on them, they shift again until he is left frustrated and confused.

After the first dream fades, he sees himself skateboarding down the street. He feels the crunch of asphalt under the wheels and the wind tickling his face. He's coasting down the big hill near his house when something blocks his path. A sea of gray gelatinous blobs are stuck to the road, their blubber baking in the afternoon sun. They remind him of the jellyfish he saw when his class took that field trip to the coast, jiggling like Jello in the sand.

The blobs all have faces, or rather, they all have the same face. Dozens of heads of thick, brown hair nest above sad eyes, and scowling lips. These faces are supported by thick necks covered in angry razor-burn bumps, their jowls quivering in quiet disappointment.

The boy wants to run away, but he knows he isn't allowed.

Julian got into an argument with his aunt the next morning and tried to hide me under his bed. I spent the day crammed alongside discarded Happy Meal toys, an overdue library book on Roman history, and several bits of long-forgotten Halloween chocolate that had petrified into a chalky white. I didn't like it. It reminded me of Clementine's trunk.

But I wasn't down there long. It was his mother who rescued me from that purgatory and once again lifted me to my place over Julian's window.

Carolyn seemed kind. She wore a patched denim jacket over a breezy summer dress. She like to sing The White Stripes as she swept the floors and searched the ceiling for stray cobwebs. I saw her every morning as she circled the house, opening windows, and every evening as she came back to close them.

She probably only put me on display for her sister's sake, but I didn't mind. I liked the company.

Tonight, he's an owl, soaring over a forest of pine and sequoia. His eyes pierce the darkness, searching for prey in the moonlight. He notices a burning orange glow that rises out of the canopies. The wind carries the scent of smoke and the sound of drums. He is afraid.

Then the dream shifts. A pink tide washes over him. It's warm and safe. He sleeps to the gentle *thra-dum, thra-dum, thra-dum,* carried on the tide.

Now he's a great Caesar, with legions of Roman centurions at his command. He takes the steps to the hall of Ptolemy, followed by a great Triumph in his honor. Flower petals rain from the sky as the people celebrate his defeat of the tyrant Mark Antony.

Cleopatra stands at the summit, ready to crown him king. Julian wonders why—beneath her bell-like hair and gold-embroidered robes—she's wearing a pair of pink high-top sneakers with the laces done up in Xs, the way the girls do them at school.

I saw Julian's parents come into his room the next afternoon to tell him about the divorce. He wondered why they told him to sit on the bed instead of letting him draw with his new colored pencils. His mom straightened her skirt and his dad scratched nervously at the red bumps that covered his neck. They sat on either side of him, each putting an arm around his narrow shoulders as they told him the papers were signed and that neither of them could afford the house on their own. They told him they would each be moving to smaller apartments, but that they were going to stay close, so it would be easy for him to see both of them as much as he wanted.

I watched them cling to him, both of them desperately trying to hold him. They thought they wanted to comfort him, but what they really wanted was for him to comfort them. They wanted him to cry or maybe even scream. Then they wanted him to hug them, and tell them that everything would be alright... that he would still love them... that they hadn't damaged him.

Instead, he froze. He didn't protest their groping, but it didn't touch him.

He's sitting in a field under the stars. A woman is with him, her arms curled into a faded blue jean jacket.

"Everything's going to be alright," she says, but this worries him.

"Why wouldn't it be?" he asks. Hadn't things always been fine before?

But she only repeats herself. "Everything's going to be alright."

He starts to get nervous and climbs to his feet. His shoes sink into the ground. The field is muddier than he thought. He tries to pull one of them loose, but it feels stuck.

"Everything's going to be alright," the woman repeats, but she isn't a woman anymore. She's transformed into a giant worm. Her body is a slimy mass of rippling tumor. Her face is gone, except for a gnarled mouth with row after row of needle-sharp teeth, spinning in her circular jaw like a coffee grinder.

He tries to run, but every step is so slow.

He's at the bottom of the ocean. He can see the beams of light, slicing through waves and currents, bending in the water. The air in his lungs is dwindling. He thinks about taking a breath, letting go and swallowing the water, falling into the void.

I keep that one from him.

I watched him pack his room, the books and toys, clothes and trinkets. He didn't take me off the wall. He didn't even look at me. I honestly wondered if he even noticed I was there. I wished I could call out to tell him that I'd seen his pain. I wanted him to know he doesn't have to suffer his nights alone. I was here for him.

I could see the moving truck out the window. They packed it to the brim with lives, soon to be divided. I wished I could move. I wanted to jump off the wall and roll my way out the door and up the ramp onto that truck. I would tuck myself between his mother's state quarter collection and his father's unused exercise weights.

But then Julian came back and looked around the empty room. His eyes caught on the shadow of my web and glazed over as he took in the splintered silhouette of his dreams. He pulled me off the wall, weighing me in his hands and trying to decide whether to throw me in the trash. I didn't blame him for thinking I was junk, but it was still a relief when he tucked me into the box of things that would soon be part of his new life.

There were more nightmares to come. I couldn't take them all. But tonight, at least, Julian would have good dreams.

He's walking through a forest. The path twists and bends, splitting in a dozen different directions, but he isn't afraid. His feet know the way.

He's humming a song that he doesn't quite remember, content in the curiosity of half-forgotten summers, vibrating on the back of his tongue.

He's starting to feel tired but clicks his feet when the trail comes to a head. He can see his home just through the trees, glowing in the sun.

He is safe.

BONES OF THE GIANT

Tick slept inside the body of a giant. Not a living giant—those died out years ago. She lived in one of the rusted metal exoskeletons that the creatures left behind. Her older brother Lance told her about the days when the massive steel men walked the Earth, herding people, and killing them when they didn't do as they were told. He spun stories to her about how they ate bones and drank thick, black oil from deep beneath the Earth.

Tick loved Lance, but she could never quite bring herself to believe his tales. Her giant had a kind face. The rivets that welded on his metal jaw twisted like dimples where its cheeks would be, making the creature wear a look similar to that of a child as he slept, of smug joy in the certainty of his own importance. It was an innocent smile, which didn't match her brother's description of the mechanical monsters that terrorized their ancestors.

There was also the matter of the giant's heart, which was three times as wide as the trunk of a fully-grown pine, and still warm, long after the decades had turned its mind to stone, and its skin to rusted iron. This was the cleverest thing about living in a giant. It meant their home always had heat, even during the winter rains, when it was all but impossible to keep wood dry. Tick didn't believe that anything with a heart so big and warm could possibly do the things Lance said.

She touched it for luck every morning on her way out the door, as she headed into the forest to check her traps. Each day that she got home safely made the metal heart feel that much more sacred.

That's why it was so frustrating that Tick couldn't recall if she'd completed her ritual that morning. She remembered waking up, putting on her clothes, and eating breakfast, but then it was a blur. She could vaguely picture herself pressing her palm against the warm metal. But did she actually do it today, or was she simply remembering one of the other countless times she'd made her luck? She'd done it so many times, on so many days, that she couldn't be sure if the memory could be trusted.

"Well, it's too late to worry about it now," she scolded herself. "You've come too far to go back."

She tried to put the heart out of her mind, but not knowing if she'd touched it was like not knowing if she'd put on underwear. It made her feel uneasy.

She checked the first trap and found it empty. The bait had been eaten away by something that wasn't big enough to set it off. It might have been ants in the summer, but beetles were the more likely culprits now that autumn had blanketed the ground in the wet leaves they loved to scurry through. Annoyed, Tick smeared more of the sweet-smelling paste she used as a lure on the release mechanism and then got to her feet. Her brother had the traps spread out a lot further back when he was around. He spent most of the day circling the forest and baiting them, sometimes coming home with more meat than they knew what to do with. All the work fell to Tick now, though.

The first thing she did after he left was to move the traps closer. She checked them once in the morning, and sometimes again in the late afternoon if there was still enough light when she'd finished her other chores. She didn't get nearly as much meat as Lance, but then, she only needed enough for one.

She came on the second trap a few minutes later. It was empty as well. Cursing under her breath, Tick reached for the tin where she kept her bait when a scream cut through the trees. The desperate, terrified cry sent birds screeching into the sky.

Tick's legs were moving before she had the chance to properly think. She knew what her brother would say if he found out that she ran *toward* the sound of screaming. He spent years drilling the dangers of meeting strangers in the woods into her long before he ever let her join him on his expeditions.

The cry was coming from a hollow, formed where the river had carved the dirt out from under the roots of a large oak. Tick came out of the woods at the top of a ridge overlooking the eroded basin. A boy was down there, clutching his leg and trying desperately to tuck himself behind the roots of the washed-out tree. A pack of wolves slowly loped their way down the opposite hill.

Tick usually avoided wolves. Her brother explained to her that they weren't like dogs. They weren't bred to love and obey humans. Wolves were wild. Their eyes were full of mistrust and predatory cunning. Lance said they had a dog when she was little named Clipper. The Aussie used to belong to Papa, but they'd been forced to eat her in Tick's third winter when there hadn't been enough food. Wolves were smarter.

They were getting closer to the boy now. It was clear the roots weren't going to protect him. Tick knew she had to act quickly if she was going to help. She looked around the clearing for the tools she would need. There were plenty of heavy-looking river stones. That was good, but she wanted something to defend herself with as well. Searching the branches of the nearby trees, she saw several thick limbs that would work as clubs. None of them had enough foliage for what she had in mind, though. Then she saw exactly what she needed. The branch had already fallen to the ground, so she wouldn't even need to worry about breaking it off the tree. It was long and slender enough that she could carry it, but one end was thick with pine needles, making it nearly big enough to cover her entire body. Tucking the branch loftily under her left arm, Tick used her free hand to pick up several of the flat river stones. The wolves were almost on him now. There wasn't much time. Tick sucked in a deep breath, filling her lungs to the point they hurt, before letting it all out in a long, loud bellow that sent dozens more birds flitting away into the morning sun. The sound was deep and threatening. It was a battle cry, intended to blast the bravery out of anything that heard it.

The wolves looked up. Their cunning eyes were startled into doubt by the newcomer. The two smallest ones even backed up a little, though their leader was still baring his teeth. He was an old wolf, nearly twice the size of the others. Bald strips of scar tissue sliced through his thick gray fur. The most prominent of them were three long, parallel grooves on his side. The only animal Tick knew that had a claw big enough to do that was a bear.

Tick raised the branch above her head. She waved it back and forth to make herself look like a giant beast, shouting her challenge as she did. That would have been enough most of the time, but these wolves were hungry. They didn't run.

Tick started throwing her stones. The first landed on a patch of dirt that was closer to the boy than any of the wolves, but her second stone hit one of the larger ones square in the shoulder. The creature made a high, yelping sound and then ran away. Most of the others followed suit, sprinting out of the clearing after their injured brother.

The leader lingered. He looked up at Tick with the pale eyes of a hunter. She knew there wouldn't be anything she could do if he chose to attack her, but without his pack, the old wolf turned and slowly padded out of the clearing to find the others.

"You alright?" Tick called to the boy. He didn't answer.

She slid down the hill, careful not to hurt herself. The last thing she needed was for both of them to be injured when the wolves came back.

And they would come back. Tick was sure of it.

The boy was about her age, maybe a little older. He was tall and gangly. His clothes were patched in places, but the parts that weren't spattered in mud looked clean and well cared for. His upper lip had just started to grow the soft, fuzzy facial hair that her brother had worn in his younger years. Tick smacked him across the face a couple of times, trying to get him to wake up, but the boy didn't so much as flutter his pretty lashes.

Tick sighed. She didn't think she could carry him, so she laid her branch on the ground and rolled the boy onto it, deciding to use the severed tree limb as a makeshift sled. Getting out of the hollow was the hardest part. It took all her strength to get his unconscious body over the muddy lip of the riverbank. The trip home was almost entirely downhill after that. But even so, her muscles ached with the effort of dragging him. She had to stop several times to take a drink of water and catch her breath.

She'd yank out one of the boy's fuzzy mustache hairs every once in a while, or else stick a finger in his ear in an attempt to agitate him into waking up, but he slept through it all like one of the princesses from her brother's old stories. Did that mean she would have to kiss him to wake him up? Tick decided to leave that as a last resort.

She worried that he might already be dead and that she'd wasted her effort in rescuing a corpse. She licked her finger and stuck it under the boy's nose and was pleased to discover that she could feel his breath, tickling against the wet skin.

He didn't rouse until they were nearly home. A large tree root crossed the path, forcing Tick to yank the boy over it. She heard a low groan from behind her as her pine branch sled thudded back onto the ground. It was the first sound he'd made since she heard him screaming for his life. She turned around to find him blinking in the late morning light, his hands pressed firmly to his temples.

"Good, you're awake," Tick said. She helped him sit upright and offered him her water skin. "My arms feel like they're about to fall off."

"Who are you?" he asked. The boy accepted the skin but gave it a suspicious sniff before drinking a small, delicate sip. He had long brown hair that almost hid the gorgeous amber-green of his eyes. Tick noticed though.

"I'm the one who saved your butt is who I am. Dragged you across half the territory too. I'm Galahad, Queen of the Nile, and Lord God Almighty as far as you're concerned."

"Galahad?" he asked, rubbing his pretty eyes with a dirt-smudged palm, "Nile? I don't know what you're talking about."

"Just stuff from books. I like to read."

"Oh, well thanks, I guess."

Tick shrugged, smiling a little.

Lance used to trade with the village, but he never brought her along. She'd only ever seen the people who lived there from a distance. She was brimming with questions but she didn't want him to think that she was ignorant, so she kept them bottled up.

The boy's eyes suddenly widened in alarm, as if he'd just realized that he'd swallowed poison. He jumped to his feet, almost falling over, but catching himself against a nearby tree.

"The wolves!" he shouted. "There were wolves following me!"

"I know," Tick replied, picking up her water skin from where he'd dropped it and brushing away the dirt and crumpled leaves. "I scared them off. I thought your brain was addled. I was taking you back to mine so that I could keep you safe until you woke up, or I could get you a doctor. You seem pretty spry now though. I guess you just needed to sleep it off."

The boy didn't respond. He just looked around at the surrounding trees, as if he expected the beasts to jump out from behind them and finish their hunt.

"They're gone," Tick reassured him. "You got a name?"

"Umm, yeah. It's George."

Tick smiled. She liked the name. It was a king's name.

"Pleasure to meet you, George," she replied, holding out her hand. "My name's Tick."

"Tick?" he asked, taking her hand. His palm was warm and dusty. The clay from the hollow beneath the tree had hardened and cracked on his skin. "I thought you said it was Galahad?"

"I was joking," she laughed. "He's a knight from a book my brother used to read me."

"Well, what kind of name is Tick?"

"My name."

The air between them grew quiet. Tick heard the soft rustling of insects scurrying beneath the leaves. Frustration started to bubble inside her. This wasn't going the way she'd imagined. She'd pictured him waking up in her home, covered in warm furs and thanking her for saving him as she spooned hot soup into his mouth. He would be so grateful and would tell her everything she wanted to know about the village while she nursed him back to health. *That's* how it was supposed to go.

"I have food," she said. "I'm sure you'll be wanting to get home, but you should eat something first, shouldn't you? It's not far."

George smiled, and Tick noticed with approval that he also had healthy-looking teeth.

"I could eat," he said.

The two of them started walking, leaving the half-destroyed branch on the trail. Tick watched him at first, to make sure that he wasn't going to fall over. She was still a little worried that his brain might have been knocked around and he could collapse again at any moment.

"So how did you end up running into a pack of wolves all by yourself anyway?" she asked, partially because she was curious, but mostly to keep the silence away. "I didn't think people from the village went into the woods alone."

"I was looking for my sister's cat," he said. "The stupid thing was always running into the woods, bringing back mice and lizards, stuff like that. I tracked it to a stream where I'd found it before, thinking I'd grab the dumb animal and drag it back, but Poppy was dead when I got there. They'd pulled her apart."

George paused for a moment. His face lost some of its color as the memory played through his mind.

"They were all just standing there," he continued. "I walked right into them like an idiot. Then they all looked up and I just about ruined my pants with fear. So, I ran. Next thing I know, I'm waking up covered in mud and scrapes, and being dragged through the woods by some girl telling me to call her God."

"Running was your mistake," Tick said. "Wolves always chase you when you run. They can't help it. It's best to stand still. Try to look big, and scare them off."

"Is that what you did?"

She nodded, shifting the shoulder strap of her empty satchel a little higher. The bag kept trying to slip off, since it didn't have so much as a rabbit to weigh it down.

"My brother taught me."

"Is he back at your place, then? I'll have to thank him for the lesson that saved my life."

"He's not home right now."

"Oh? Where is he then? Off hunting?"

"He went to look for another village," she said. "Someone told him there was one on the river down south. He was going to go find it, then come back for me."

"How long has he been gone?"

"He left about mid-spring. He promised to find it and come back before the rains started."

"But spring ended months ago," George said quietly. "Autumn is nearly over. The rains are going to start any day."

"I know that," Tick spat back at him. She was starting to get annoyed. She saved the stupid boy's life, after all. What right did he have to tell her how long Lance had been gone? Didn't he think she knew? The sky had been gray for weeks.

"Sorry," he said, turning his eyes back toward the path. "I just meant that I hope he gets back soon."

"Yeah, me too. It's been hard without him. He used to be in charge of the traps. Now I have to do it on top of all my other work."

"I'm surprised he went by himself. Why didn't one of your parents go with him?"

"No parents. It's just me and Lance."

"You live out here by yourself?" he asked.

"Me and Lance," she corrected.

"But how do you—" he started, but Tick never heard what he was going to ask.

They had just ducked under the low-hanging branches that covered the trail's entrance and were standing under the sleeping gaze of her giant. The metal man had his back pressed up against a hill. His legs were sprawled out in front of him while his arms lay crooked over his thighs. Tick could have fit her whole body in his foot, but the doorway her brother cut into their home was located in the left hip.

George's face turned as pale as a rain-soaked worm. His pretty eyes looked like they were trying to pop out of their sockets as they took in the colossal figure in the foreground.

"Tha-that's a giant," he stammered.

"I know. I live here."

"We need to run," he said, already starting to back away. He shuffled into the low-hanging branches that they'd just ducked under, letting out a little cry of surprise as the twigs prodded against his back. "We need to go now."

"Don't worry," Tick said laughing. "It's been dead for a hundred years."

But George wasn't listening.

He ducked under the branches and started running back the way they came, toward where the wolves attacked him.

"Come on," he shouted, but he didn't turn back to make sure she was following. The sound of his footsteps was gone in seconds.

Tick just stood there for a moment in stunned silence. She waited, thinking that George would eventually turn back. Maybe he would come back smiling, as if he'd only run away as a joke. Or perhaps he would return with his cheeks burning in embarrassment when he realized how foolish his reaction had been? But he didn't. He was just gone.

Tick could hardly believe it. She'd saved him. She'd pulled him out of the jaws of death and dragged him almost the entire way here. How could he just leave like that? Suddenly the name George didn't seem very kingly at all.

She looked at her giant. The shade cast by the trees in the late afternoon sun hid his wry smile, making him look sad.

Then she started to cry. Tick was used to being by herself, but that also meant there was no one to hold back her tears for. She'd long since learned to let them out when they started to flow and have done with it.

She was still sobbing as she climbed the ladder into her giant's chest and crawled into the small oak bed, nestled beside its heart.

Why had she bothered to save the coward? She should have just left him to get eaten.

She kept picturing the fear on George's face when he looked at her magnificent giant. She realized that Lance used to look at it the same way. She remembered the way her brother's lips would curl in disgust as he glared at the gargantuan husk of the ancient automaton. Tick knew that he only allowed them to stay there out of pragmatism. He hated the giant, but he never ran.

Tick always thought Lance was just being silly, though. It was his idea for them to move into the giant's used-up shell after the infection killed their papa. Tick was so little back then that most of her memories were a blur. She had a hard time remembering anything before moving into the steel man. Sometimes when she closed her eyes and thought about it, she saw a small camp that smelled of smoke and tanned leather. She remembered a wall of stacked pine for firewood that also hid reserves of seeds, nuts, and dried roots. Sometimes she remembered being held by her papa. She recalled being nestled in the crook of a warm, fleshy arm, staring up at his face and cooing as he rocked her. Every once in a while, there would be a flash of light against steel as he chipped away at the wood with the other arm—the one made of cold metal. She wasn't sure if this memory was real, or just something she'd made up after listening to her brother's stories, but it didn't matter.

It was Lance who raised her. He was the one who fed her and took care of her for as long as she could remember. Their papa wasn't allowed in the village because of his prosthetic. People were afraid of the metal men. They were so scared that even people like her papa, who only had metal parts, weren't allowed anywhere near their settlement. Tick wondered about them sometimes. She agreed with her brother that they were stupid for casting their father out just because he didn't have both his arms, but she couldn't bring herself to hate them the way Lance did. He was willing to spend every day living inside a thing he despised, just so he wouldn't have to go back to them.

Tick pulled the furs tight around her shoulders until the shaking stopped. Then she got up. The sun hadn't even started to set. She couldn't spend the day moping. She had too much work to do.

Tick didn't come back to her bed until long after dark. She'd chopped some wood, gathered some blackberries from the riverside, and used one of her older animal skins to patch up a rusty hole in the giant's head so it wouldn't leak when the rains came. Her muscles felt like they'd been replaced with lead when she finally hit the soft mattress. She didn't think that anything in the world could move her before morning. She reached with a clumsy arm to the shelf over her bed. There were fourteen books stacked on its surface. She'd read them all many times and could tell each of them apart by feel. She knew she'd found the one she was looking for when her fingers brushed its beveled spine. Her copy of *A Wrinkle in Time* was old and weathered. The book's paper jacket was so worn that you could barely read the title. Several of the pages had fallen out of the binding and were simply tucked back into place.

Like everything else in her life, it was Lance who taught her to read.

"People wrote these," he'd said when he first showed her his precious collection. "They took the stories in their heads and put them on paper so other people could hear them too—even after the writers were dead. Books are living proof that people didn't always used to be so stupid."

She'd read this one more than any of the others. It was her favorite, so she always found her way back to it, especially when she was feeling sad.

She was so immersed in the story that it took her a few minutes to realize that the crickets outside were no longer chirping. A dead silence had fallen around her giant. It was so quiet that the sound of claws clicking against steel cut through the night's stillness as sharply as if someone had banged a drum.

Tick edged out of bed, keeping herself wrapped tightly in her furs. She was careful not to make a sound as she crept to the door on the giant's hip.

There was a flash of movement as an animal sniffed its way between Tick and the dim light cast by the moon. She stifled a gasp of surprise and ducked away from the door.

Of course they'd followed her. Wolves were hunters by nature. They were good at tracking wounded animals, and she'd nearly dragged George to her doorstep. She may as well have left a trail of meat for them to follow.

There was another bookcase beside the entrance, though this one was full of tools and harvesting equipment instead of paperbacks. It was made of heavy, mismatched wood. Her brother repaired the pegs and cut new shelves of fresh pine after he found the casing. She grabbed the small pair of shears she'd used to collect the berries earlier that day, holding them close to her chest. She hadn't cleaned them yet, so the juice still stained the blades a gory shade of purple.

There wasn't another way into the giant from the ground. She would be safe if she cut them off here. Her only hope was to push the shelf over and pray it would be enough to keep the wolves from getting inside.

Tick braced her back against the side of the heavy shelf, but her breath caught in her throat when she tried to push. What if she wasn't strong enough to knock it over and the wolves heard her? Would she be better off hiding instead? What if the shelf shattered? The casing was old. Who knew how strong it was? That would attract their attention and leave the entrance wide open.

She pictured herself pinned down by the leader, his pincer-like fangs holding her by the neck as his pack tore at her skin.

Tick shook the thought out of her head, though she couldn't stop her hands from trembling. She crouched, anchoring her shoulder as firmly as she could. Then, using the strong muscles in her legs, she took a deep breath and heaved against the wall of shelves as hard as she could.

At first, she thought it wasn't going to budge, but then the corner by her foot lifted the tiniest bit as she strained against it. She reached down with her free hand, grabbing the lifted corner and leveraging the weight of the shelf over the opposite side.

It fell with a bombastic crash that shook the giant's hull. Tick tumbled after it, catching herself painfully on the sharp bottom edge she'd used to flip it. She turned to look at the entrance. The shelf covered most of it, but there was a small gap at the top.

Almost at once, the leader's head appeared in the gap. His long nose was wrinkled into a death snarl. The scars that cross-crossed his face shined like oil in the moonlight.

The beast clawed and bit at the shelf, scraping at it with his paws. Tick grabbed her shears and charged at the wolf, aiming for his eye, but the pack master was too quick for her. He twisted his mouth around her wrist before she could blind him and clamped down with curved teeth that went straight to the bone. She dropped the shears. The beast shook his head and Tick could feel warm blood streaming from her wrist to her shoulder and soaking into the fur she'd wrapped herself in.

An idea struck her through the pain and panic. She grabbed the pelt from her shoulders and wrapped it around the wolf's head. Confused, the beast released her, and she fell back to the ground. The pack master retreated from the hole.

Tick picked up the sheers from where they'd fallen. She put them in her left hand since her right was still bleeding and crouched, ready to attack.

Pain was screaming in her head. Part of her was crying out for George, Lance, or her papa to come and save her. Luckily, the adrenalin coursing through her system helped to push those unhelpful thoughts down. This left her mind free to race through a dozen contingencies for how she would survive the night.

Should she run? No. There was only one other way out and that was more likely to get her killed than the wolves. She couldn't kill them all. Maybe if she could kill one while it was trying to get through, it would plug up the gap and the others wouldn't be able to fit. That could work, but she'd have to be fast. She only had one hand left.

Tears flooded down her face as she raised the shears, waiting for the next creature to stick his head in. The pain radiating from her wrist seemed to demand her attention. Waves of nausea washed over her as she started slipping into shock. She worried about how much blood she was losing, but she didn't dare take her eyes off the gap above the bookcase. The beast never came, though.

Instead, the giant's body lurched as if an earthquake had broken it free from the hillside. Tick could hear a rusty groan, rattling through the narrow halls of its limbs as it moved. The ground beneath her feet tilted this way and that, making it impossible for Tick to keep her footing. She tumbled to the floor, where she rolled around with the discarded tools from the collapsed shelf. Then there was a percussive thump of something heavy hitting the dirt outside, immediately followed by the high whine of an animal in pain. The groaning grew louder and a wall of metal sealed off all the light that had been filtering through the giant's hip. She felt the giant's body sway back and forth, and then it went still.

Tick heard the distant thunder of padded feet as they skittered off into the distance. Then there was silence once again.

She decided that finding some light was the first thing she needed to do as soon as she was certain the floor wouldn't start moving again. Then she washed her arm and used the last of her clean linens to bandage it.

It started to rain after the wolves were gone. Tick spent the night listening to the droplets ping against her giant's metal body, hoping bitterly that the animals were soaked through before they made it back to their den. The pattering sound was sad, but Tick didn't have any more tears to give to the rain.

Tick found a way out of the giant in the morning. The hip-door was blocked, and she didn't have the tools to cut a new one, so she climbed up to the automaton's head and shoved out his eye. The wolves would have certainly heard the clattering glass ball as it shattered on the metal man's chest if she'd tried to get out this way the night before—even if she didn't break her neck trying to climb down in the dark. But now the sun was up and this was the only way she could think to escape.

Gathering her few remaining valuables—her dried meat, her furs, and her books—Tick touched the cool engine of the giant's heart. Then she slowly climbed out of his eye socket and down his torso until she finally reached the ground.

But she noticed something strange as she looked back at the metal man that had been her home. It wasn't where it used to be. She hadn't been imagining it. The machine's arms were crossed. They were wrapped around its stomach as if it had a tummy ache, with its hands covering its hips. The ground looked different as well. There were large trenches of black dirt through the moss and leaves where the giant's massive elbows had been resting. Its face had changed too, and not just because of the missing eye. It now wore a scowl of grim determination, its metal jaw set over its mouth like a bulldog.

It was alive. There had been the tiniest bit of power left after all these years and the giant used it to protect her. She wanted to kiss her big, beautiful, gallant friend, but there was no life left in it now. The rains had finally come, and Tick was completely alone. She hoped that her brother was okay, wherever he was, but she decided that she was done waiting.

Slowly, Tick gathered her things and started down the trail that led to the village, the heart of a giant beating within her.

CROSSING OVER

It tasted like blood, only thicker. And something else... chalk? The big man in the romper warned me to plug my nose. I should've listened. He seemed nice for a border wrangler. Didn't feel me up or nothing, just told me I had to drink it all and he had to watch to make sure that I did. I could see my mom through the glass. Her hair was in knots. She was crying, but I didn't know why. It's not like she had to drink anything.

My brothers said they drank it all in one go, but Mom says they're full of it. She says it took Billy near twenty minutes and Jacob gagged so hard she thought he was going to blow. My stomach felt like it was full of snakes, but I didn't want the border wrangler to see me turning green. I heard they don't let you through if you puke. My glass was more than half empty now. I steeled my belly, plugged my nostrils, and swallowed the rest. It's a good thing I was hungry.

Billy says the Northers give you food every day. Jacob says that too, but he says it's just donuts all the time. I tell Jacob I like donuts. He says I do now, but I'll start to hate them once I've been eating fried dough for every meal, even when they give me jellies, which he knows are my favorite.

They say you can get water for free from taps on the street that don't give you the runs and the Northers make sure you got somewhere warm to be on frosty nights. They might be lying, but like Mom says, "anythin' is better than nothin'"

I told my friend Cricket back in the States about the donuts, and his mouth started watering like a busted pipe. His name wasn't always Cricket, but that's what we took to calling him when he got his arms blown off.

"You'll write me every day, won't you?" he asked, bouncing on his heels.

"Well sure, Crick, but how's you gonna write me back?"

"I'll have my mom do it," he scoffed. "Just take care of yourself over there, Poll. I'm happy you're getting out."

"You will too, just give it time," I said.

He nodded, but we both knew it was a lie. The Northers only let healthy people cross. Cricket and his parents were stuck, and that meant they'd probably be dead soon. I still meant to write the letters, though. People acted like the stuck ones was already dead, but they weren't.

Once my glass was licked clean, the border wrangler took me by the arm and pulled me through to the next room. Mom had to say behind. I saw her waving through the window before the doors swung shut.

It felt darker in here. The floor was wet, like at the car wash. The room was empty except for a hose. The wrangler pointed at a clothes hook and told me to strip down to my undies. I looked into his eyes and was glad to see that he was uncomfortable, too. There's a hunger in some people that you have to watch out for.

The water was icy. It bit like a hornet wherever he pointed. I had to force myself to think about how many people would kill to be where I am. I shook with my hands pressed against the wall, reminding myself how lucky I was, over and over, until it was done. Then he handed me a hospital gown.

"Put that on now," he said. "Carry your clothes into Med-Eval. You can wear them again when you're done."

The next room stank like a public pool. Everything was lit up in the way you expect heaven to be, all white and shiny, so you could see the dark brown stains in the corners that were hard for mops to reach. Doctors in white coats were walking around with needles. Two of them, an old one and a young one, came over when the wrangler brought me in.

"Did you finish the barium?" the young one asked. He looked like a kid playing dress up, couldn't've been much older than Billy.

"Yessir," I said, keeping my eyes on my feet like Momma taught me.

"All of it?" asked the older man. He had a beard, sheared tight to fit his sour face. "Don't waste our time if you didn't. We'll know."

I nodded, and they took me over to what looked like a bed with a camera attached to it. There weren't any blankets or pillows, but there were thick leather straps that dangled off the edges like snakes.

"Lie down, keep your arms at your sides, and for God's sake, don't move," said the older man.

Momma told me not to ask questions, but I couldn't help myself. "What's it do?"

"It's going to make sure you aren't hiding anything in there," he said, poking me in the belly with a bony finger. "Sick people are expensive and smugglers get the boot."

I looked at the contraption and pictured the glass eye of the camera, squinting at me. I shivered as I imagined a cold metal hand probing around in my stomach, searching blindly for lumps and sores, weapons and pouches of powder.

"Don't worry," the young one said. "It won't hurt. Just hold real still and it'll all be over in a minute."

"These tests would have cost a fortune state-side," the older man said. "You should be thanking us."

"Thank you," I said.

It was blue skies after that. The machine must've told them I wasn't sick because they gave me my clothes back and sent me outside; the North side. I've never been passed the border before. I was a little disappointed. It seemed like the sky should be a different color — like the air should taste different — but it all seemed pretty much the same. A group of birds passed over the border wall as I looked up, flying in the shape of a giant V.

Dad used to joke back in the safe days that he didn't marry Mom for citizenship, but it was definitely a perk. He hated growing up in Canada. He said if it weren't rainy, it was about to snow. Then he went out to buy Mom a new hairdryer when the bad stuff started and got shot. Mom's been trying to get us here ever since. We've had a couple of other dads since then, but he was the best one.

"Polly!" Jacob shouted. He rushed through the crowd of people who were blinking like newborns in the northern sun and pulled me up into a warm hug. I let myself relax into it, unclenching muscles I didn't know I had.

"About time," Billy said, appearing beside him. They both had dad's dark hair and smile. People used to say they could've been twins if Billy weren't two years older. Then the Firsties tried to recruit him.

He said no, so they branded his cheek with the star-spangled shield. Sometimes his bad eye cries when he ain't sad. No one mixes them up anymore. "We've been waiting for hours. Thought the Firsties might've got you."

"Nobody gettin' me," I said, smiling. "I'm a Norther now."

"Well, not quite, mon ami," said an older lady with a thick accent. She had beautiful, dark hair that looked too young for her face. I could smell her perfume even in the crowd, like dried roses and rubbing alcohol. "We need to get you settled first."

"Who're you?" I asked.

"This is our Aunt Priscilla," said Billy. "She's Dad's sis'. We're staying with her."

"Come along," she said, looking around nervously at the shivering refugees. "Your uncle Joe is waiting at home. We can talk more in the car."

"What about Mom?" I asked.

"She did not tell you? Your mother cannot come across yet," Aunty Priscilla said, hugging herself. Her eyes kept darting around at the squinting faces. "Your father was a Canadian, which makes you and your brothers Canadian. Your mother is a citizen of the States, so it's going to take her a little longer to get the visa. She has to work on her French."

"French?"

"Oui, if you are not a Canadian citizen, you must learn French to become one. Come now, into the car."

She led us to a little gray sedan. It was a tight fit, but it was cleaner and more comfortable than anything I was used to. Hot air blew out of a vent by my feet.

"Look at them all," Aunty Priscilla said, glaring out the window at a clump of people crowding around a fire. She seemed like she was talking to herself more than to any of us. "They let more in every day, don't they? How can they possibly be screening them all?"

"What they screening for?" Jacob asked.

"Trying to keep out as many Southies as they can," Billy said from the front seat.

"No, no," Aunty Priscilla said. "Just the bad people. You know, les dangereux? We know that some of you are good, but as they say, rotten apples spoil the bunch."

The house was bonkers. Way bigger than our old apartment. It lived out in the woods on the edge of town, surrounded by trees. It was raining when we got there, so we all had to leave our shoes on a special mat with grooves in it to dry them out. The walls were decorated with framed rips of cloth that had pictures stitched in the middle. The floor was wood, so it was cold without shoes, even though a fire cracked behind a metal shield. But there was even weirder stuff in the living room. There were little wooden statues of birds scattered all over. They looked like ducks, but their beaks were pointy. Clocks were on every wall, ticking heavy so the sound bounced around the room like hammers on springs.

The house had two bedrooms. There was the big one where Aunty Priscilla and Uncle Joe slept, and the little one they turned into a room for the boys and me. It had a big heavy bed that was made of old wood and a bunk bed made of blue metal that smelled like oil and plastic. I asked Aunty Priscilla if her and my uncle had kids, but she said no. She said Uncle Joe had a congenial brain deficit and they didn't think it was fair to pass it on. Then he went and had a stroke two years ago. They bought the bunk bed for us.

Billy got the big bed cause he's the oldest, but I had to wrestle Jacob for the top bunk. He's bigger and stronger than me, but I whoop him anyway because he always holds back. He cried until I told him we could share it after I rubbed his nose into the floorboards. I wasn't sure I was ready to have my own bed yet anyways.

One thing I did like about the house was the pond out back. At least, Aunty Priscilla called it a pond. It was ten times the size of the house, which made it more like an ocean if you asked me. Uncle Joe spent most days sitting on a bench out there watching the geese. He didn't talk, but he was good company.

The geese were brown and white and shiny black. They'd strut around with webbed toes as if they owned every inch of mud some-times. But they were usually out on the water, floating on their reflec-tions. Every once in a while, one would let loose a strangled cry that reminded me of the sound people make right before they die. They were funny.

Aunty let me use her desk to write up my letter to Cricket that night after dinner.

"Just remember," she said, smiling. "No matter how far you push the envelope, it's still stationary."

She smiled and I could tell she was trying to make a joke. I didn't get it, but I laughed anyway.

The paper was thick and clean. For a moment, I was scared to get ink on it. My brain was fuzzy from all the food. I had to shake my head to keep from nodding off.

Finally, I pushed the pen onto the paper and wrote "Dear Cricket," at the top.

The words were ugly and crooked. I tried thinking of what to put next, but nothing jumped out. I wanted to tell him about the crossing and about Mom staying behind. I wanted to tell him how weird it was here and how I felt like crying, even though I didn't know why. I wanted to try and explain the wrongness I felt, deep in my belly, but I didn't think I had a right to complain—poor Cricket still being stuck like he was.

Frustrated, I put that sheet off to the side. I wouldn't waste good paper, but I wanted to wait till I had more to tell him. I started a new letter to Momma instead.

Dear Mom,

Me and Jacob and Billy got to Aunty Priscilla's alright. I wish you told me you weren't coming. I would have said goodbye. Why didn't you?

It's weird here, but the house is nice. We stopped at a restaurant on the way and they gave us fries with gravy on them. Jacob wouldn't eat any, but I had a bunch. There's a pond in the backyard with geese. I like them. Uncle Joe has a stroke, or he used to, so now he can't talk. He's kind of like our old neighbor Froggy after the police found out she fibbed; except he still has his tongue. Joe doesn't do much, but he watches geese with me, which is nice. Aunty Priscilla says you got to learn French to be a Norther. Please learn it fast so you can come soon. Jacob cries a lot.

-Polly

The next week was a rainy blur. Aunty Priscilla got us going in school. The other kids were in the middle of doing a report on animals, so I chose to do mine on the Canada Goose. I got books at the library that said they also live in the States, a bunch of them is called a gaggle, and they go south every year at wintertime—sometimes all the way to Mexico. Most of the other gaggles already left, so mine must not mind the cold much.

"Why don't you tell us a little about America, Polly?" the teacher asked one day when the class was talking about the insurgence. Twenty faces turned to look at me and the room got real quiet. I didn't know how to answer her. America seemed so big the way she talked about it.

"I don't know nothing about battles or senates or none of that," I said. "I mean, we keep our noses down around the Firsties and the police, sure, but I didn't see a lot of fighting. I mostly just helped my mom when she got jobs and played games with my brothers. You know, hide and seek? That sort of thing."

They kept looking at me. I wanted the teacher to talk again, but she wouldn't. She nodded, waiting for more. Her eyes were full of tears, like she'd never heard anything so sad. I didn't get it. I could feel my cheeks burning up with all their stares, so I said what I knew they wanted.

"I'm just grateful to be here."

I didn't get nothing in the mail from Momma when I got home, but I had a letter from Cricket. His mom wrote it in her obnoxiously smooth cursive on the back of a crumpled flier for a missing kid named Miguel. It was full of questions about Northers and asking me why I hadn't written him yet. Aunty Priscilla said I couldn't write nothing else till I did homework. There was so much of it that it took me all night, though. I had to wait till the next morning and get up early to scribble something back to him.

I told Crick about the good stuff, like the food, the clothes, the geese, and the warm fire. I decided not to tell him how dumb I felt at school, or how the other girls looked at me, laughing and whispering in French whenever the teacher wasn't looking, or how Aunty Priscilla don't know good stories like my mom used to tell us.

Once it was all sealed up, I took it down to the end of the driveway. The postbox was carved to look like a wooden moose, so you had to open his mouth to put the letters in. It wasn't a toy, even though it looked like one. The first time Aunty Priscilla got mad at me was for trying to ride it. I opened the moose's mouth to put my letter in and saw another one was already waiting in his gullet. It was a red envelope and my name was written on the front in Mom's loopy letters. I swapped them, barely remembering to put up the moose's tail before sprinting back to the house. The rain was light that morning, but I tucked the letter under my shirt to keep it safe all the same.

"Polly, is that you, mon ami?" said Aunty Priscilla as soon as the door closed behind me. Her accent sounded funnier than usual this morning. I wondered if she was getting sick.

"Yeah," I said.

"Come in here, please."

I kept the letter tucked in my shirt. I was going to share it with Billy and Jacob eventually, but it was my letter and I wanted to read it first. I went into the living room and saw Aunty Priscilla standing there. Her face was all streaky, and she had a telephone pressed against her chest. Billy and Jacob were already on the couch looking like they were each just hit in the face with a baseball bat.

"I have just heard..." she stammered. "We've just got a call from the border services. The camp where your mother was staying was just attacked by America First extremists."

My belly dropped as I realized what she was saying. I heard the words, but my brain didn't want to make sense of it. The room got swirly. The clocks bounced their ticks and tocks all over the place till the air was full of their ugly noise. My knees couldn't take the weight.

I asked if she was okay.

"Eighteen people died. Your mother... Oh mon Dieu... Your mother was one of them. They confirmed her I.D."

Jacob hucked a pillow at Aunty Priscilla and ran wailing into our tiny room. She flinched, her eyes wide in shock, and then threw herself on me in a desperate, clutching hug, moaning loudly and shaking as she pawed at my back. I stared through the gap in her arms at one of the pointy-faced wooden birds. My book said they were called loons.

"You poor thing," she said after a minute, finally letting me go. "You poor, *poor* thing. I'll make you some tea."

I said okay.

She stumbled on her way back to the kitchen, catching herself on the doorframe and then disappearing through it. I tried to think about Mom, but I found myself fixed on the loon instead. It had the kind of ridges where it ought to be smooth that told you it was hand carved. I'd never noticed before. I wondered if Uncle Joe made it. Maybe he made all the wooden things around here. I was concentrating so hard on it that I forgot Billy was still sitting on the couch.

"I don't know why we're surprised," he said, startling me.

His voice sounded weird too, like it was coming from some deep part of him he usually kept hidden away. He pulled a clean paper towel from his pocket and pressed it against his bad eye. He let his good one flow.

"They were never going to let her through," he said. "It was just a matter of time."

Then he got up, quiet as a corpse, and followed Jacob into the bedroom, leaving me alone. I didn't want to go in there with them. The crying was too real and the idea of waiting with the clocks for Aunty Priscilla to come back with tea made my belly squirm. I put my shoes back on and went out back, shuffling down the path to the pond.

Uncle Joe was sitting on his bench, staring at the geese. He didn't watch me come down the path. He didn't look at me when I stood next to him. Sometimes I wondered if he even knew I was there.

"They're leaving soon," I said, a little louder than I meant to. My throat was tight and so I had to force the words out. "What you gonna stare at when they're gone?"

Joe didn't answer, but the birds came drifting up to the water's edge. They did that when they saw me now. They knew I usually brought bread. Looking at them tightened my teeth.

"Go away," I shouted at them. "Leave if you're going! Don't act like you're gonna stay, then slip off without even saying goodbye! It's not nice to trick people!"

I pulled the letter out of my shirt, crumpled it into a ball, and chucked it as hard as I could at the big one that I called Toothy Honker. Five of them dived on it. They jabbed and shanked with their beaks, pulling bits of red and white paper from the body of it and dropping the pieces on the pond's surface to float like petals. I panicked and jumped into the water. The freezing cold sloshed up my legs while I swung my arms at the birds. They cried at my betrayal, screaming at me and beating their wings. I grabbed the biggest bits of letter and pulled them from the ice. The birds bit and slapped their breasts against the tortured water, but I was already gone.

I clutched the fragments of letter against my chest, the wet paper grabbing at my skin. Then I sat, shivering, on the bench next to Uncle Joe. The letter was probably six pages thick, but it was completely unreadable. Mom's loopy words were smeared and sticky.

"Geese," Joe wheezed.

I looked at him in surprise. It was the first word I'd heard him speak, but his face hadn't changed at all. One cheek was still all frozen, while the other sagged over.

He definitely said it, though. It wasn't my imagination.

I leaned against him and cried.

Following his eyes, I saw the birds grouping up on the far side of the pond. They'd had food and a good place to sleep here until now, but they knew it wasn't safe anymore. All together they spread their wings, giant eagle-sized things that were bigger than they had a right to. They were like angels with fat, feathered bodies and long graceful necks. Together they jumped into the sky and together they curved, floating on nothing toward someplace warm.

I've never wanted anything so badly as I wanted to go with them, but I had to remember to be grateful for where I was.

LAST OF THE LEGION

The empire has fallen. The one shimmering beacon of civilization in a world of chaos has been extinguished. I was there. I watched as Rome's crumbling bones finally succumbed to the sickness that had infected them for generations.

I've heard stories of the Rome that was. An empire whose borders stretched to the edge of the known world, spreading knowledge and philosophy like a great torch against the darkness of ignorance. But even my father's father couldn't remember the days in which the city knew its old glory. War stretched back for time beyond memory, yet no amount of blood could staunch the corruption that came from within.

I am not without guilt. I played my small part in the end of the world.

I was in the Palace of Domitian when the war council convened. I stood on the vibrantly polished stone floor, surrounded by opulent marble columns that held gilded archways. I smelled the spring breeze that passed through the open *loggia*. It carried the scent of roses from the emperor's garden as we listened to a panicked scout recite reports of Vandals raiding villages to the north. I watched as our *Magister Militum*, fat and complacent, bid our emperor to do nothing.

"Let the Goths defend themselves," he said, greasy fingers pulling the flesh from a roast bird as he spoke. "Are they not citizens of Rome? Should they not work to defend the lands upon which you so graciously allow them to reside? There is no profit in killing savages."

"They are alarmingly close, Marcus," the emperor said, his boyish face appearing mildly concerned. "They have spread deep into the west. They're all around us now. Are you certain they won't eventually make their way here?"

The magister chuckled as he shook his head, his neck wobbling. "Rome has never been taken, Dominus. Not in two millennia. It won't fall to a horde of savages. Turn your legions west. I hear Iberian grapes make for a wine that nearly rivals our own."

A steady rhythm of panic rose in my blood. I looked into the eyes of the other soldiers and saw the same fear in them that I felt rattling in my bones. The older ones had fought the Vandals in Gaul. I'd heard tales of those battlefields, though I never saw them myself. The fighting there lasted months. They say the miasma of rotting flesh baking in the summer sun was so powerful by the end that men could not breathe.

I'd fought them through the Iberian Peninsula during their push to Afrika. It was a last-ditch effort to stop their expansion that ended in failure. They fought like animals. Wave after wave of them threw themselves against our shields until we were buried beneath their corpses.

I spent two nights trapped under a mound of the dead. I couldn't move—could scarcely breathe. I thought I would join them soon and worried that my soul would not be able to escape from under so much rancid flesh. Death didn't come for me, though. Instead, I bore witness to a different horror.

Strange, foreign creatures came on the third night to eat the corpses. They prowled amid the trees and waited for nightfall to approach. I couldn't see well. It was dark, and I was half-dead with thirst, but I remember that they were large, and covered in a mange of spotted fur. I remember the sound of their jaws as they ripped apart the meat, but their laughter was worse. The noises they made turned more human with each mouthful of flesh, till they were left giggling with the stolen voices of the men they'd devoured.

I asked about them later. The locals called them crocotta.

I knew the magister was underestimating the Vandals. But I did not speak. To do so would have been to invite severe punishment on me and my family. So, I remained silent.

We all did.

It was only after the war council adjourned and I saw the legionnaires marching through the Aurelian walls several days later that I finally found my voice.

"Do not do this," I told Titus, my commander, my *centurio princeps,* as a stream of soldiers filed through the city gate to find riches in foreign lands. "I cannot defend Rome alone."

"You will do what you must, Hadrian."

"Just as two soldiers can't be expected to man a wall, you cannot expect a hundred to defend Rome."

"I've no more choice in the matter than you do," he said. "We are all the emperor's subjects. We are all at the mercy of his whims."

A shadow crossed his eyes as he spoke. Titus had been a soldier since before I was old enough to lift a stick. He'd fought the Vandals in over a dozen campaigns and has seen their slow expansion across our lands firsthand. He knew what was coming.

"There won't be an emperor if you leave," I told him. "There won't be anything."

The old soldier pushed me against a wall. He was surprisingly strong despite his gray hair and large belly. His eyes were manic and his breath smelled of wine.

"Be careful *Centurio*," he said, baring the purple stains on his teeth. "Another man might mistake your words for treason. This city has not fallen in a thousand years. It will not fall now."

I went home to my wife and daughters that night. The air was warm and carried the scent of incense from the nearby temple. Insects played their songs under the pale light of the moon. Walking down those quiet streets, I understood why the emperor didn't question his magister's lack of caution. Who could imagine that there was any force in the world that could threaten this?

When I reached my house, I saw Lavinia sitting at the table in the yard with our younger daughter Ceres propped in her lap. A violet *Paeonia*, plucked from the trellis outside our door, was nestled between the loose folds of her chestnut curls. Our oldest, Aelia, sat on the bench across from them with her arms wrapped around her skinny knees. She dipped a lump of bread in herb-infused oil and chewed it thoughtfully as they listened to Niall tell a story.

"And then Romulus heard a song," the old servant said, his voice trembling. "It was a sound said to be so sweet as to make honey taste like vinegar. And so he followed the melody until he found a woman dressed in naught but the light of the moon. She was sitting upon the corpse of a great she-wolf and running her fingers through her hair to comb out the gentle knots made by the wind." He held up an arthritic hand as if reaching out to her.

"Romulus knew the beast she sat upon. It was the very same she-wolf that he and his brother had nursed from after being sent down the Tiber. He thought it a clear sign that this woman was a gift, sent to him by the gods, and so he made her his wife.

"This worked out well for Romulus at first. You see, the woman's song was powerful. Men came from all the different tribes to help build his vision of Rome upon the Palatine hill. No one had ever seen such a construction. A mismatched rabble of farmers, tribesmen, and foreign kingdoms came together to breathe life into a city that could rival any creation of the ancient *Graeca*.

"But Romulus' brother, Remus, was jealous. They had been born together, been sent down the Tiber together to avoid the wrath of a king who wanted them dead. They had nursed from the she-wolf and grew strong enough to kill that rival king—together. He'd expected that they would rule together as well and was envious of the power this woman had given his brother.

"So, Remus devised a plan. He and Romulus were twins, you see, and clever Remus used their shared visage to trick the woman and bed her in his brother's house. He believed that his brother would be grateful to him for exposing the low character of his wife.

"But this was not so. When Romulus discovered the treachery, he killed his brother in the sheets of his bed and had the woman hauled off to the eastern mountains. He then declared the mountains forbidden so that no man would ever be tempted by her voice again."

The old man coughed when he finished speaking, and his daughter, Mila, helped his withered hands find their way to the cup of water on the table before him. Niall had been old when I first bought his services, but he'd once been a capable man. He ran my house when

I was campaigning at the edge of the world. I couldn't bring myself to make a beggar of him, even when his eyesight began to fail and his hands could scarcely grip a brush.

"That's no version of the founding I've ever heard," I said.

"Dominus," the old servant said, pushing himself shakily to his feet. "Your wife asked to hear a new tale. She said my usual stories had lost their luster. This is a version of the founding my family used to tell when I was small. I thought they might enjoy it."

Aelia took one look at me and then jumped from the bench and stormed into the house, slamming the door behind her.

"What was that about?" I asked.

"Nothing to worry over," Lavinia said, rising from the table to greet me with a kiss. "Your daughter has simply grown old enough to despise you. It happens to all children, eventually."

"Perhaps these stories of women with the power to bend men to their will are to blame. They put strange ideas in her head."

"Is that what you think that story was? It seemed to me more like a story about men who can't help but blame women for their own impotence."

"Hm, as you say."

Lavinia snorted. "It's a small wonder that you've never heard it. What man would ever acknowledge a story that says a woman built Rome?"

"Do you think the priests and philosophers would omit details from such an important tale?"

"You received your education from the Temple of Mars," she said teasingly. "The priests there try to rewrite history with almost as much enthusiasm as the Christians."

Ceres cooed and Lavinia bounced her on her hip. She was less than three summers old, and already so big that her mother could barely carry her. Golden hairs stuck to her brow with sweat. I brushed them behind her ear with my thumb and watched her face wrinkle.

Lavinia's face fall as she turned back from the babe to look at me. I realized, too late, that I'd dropped the mask which had been hiding my fear.

"What's wrong, my love?"

I looked up at Niall. I didn't want anyone else to overhear. Mila was already helping him towards the servants' house to prepare for bed.

"A horde of savages is coming to take Rome," I told her in a low voice, just above a whisper. "The *Magister Militum* has sent the army west. There won't be enough soldiers left when they get here."

"What does that mean? Will the battle reach the walls?"

"It will, and I do not believe that the walls will hold them."

Lavinia's eyes widened. She'd sat with me during the long nights after my return from the peninsula. She'd soothed me when I woke up screaming with visions of the damned and listened as I described the horrors I'd seen in that dark and distant place. I tried to keep them from her, but she insisted that bottled fear poisoned the mind, and implored me to let her bleed it. I held out for as long as I could, but I eventually conceded. Lavinia was too smart for me. Too persistent. She always got what she wanted in the end.

"You're sure?" she asked.

"The Vandals are not great military thinkers, but they will number in the tens of thousands. Even if we rally the Vigils and the Praetorian Guard to help bolster our ranks, their crude spears and arrows will eventually overwhelm us. Then they will come inside, rip the emperor from his seat, and kill what citizens they cannot take as slaves."

"What are you going to do?"

"I am a centurion. I will do my duty and die protecting Rome."

"No," she said. "Leave with us tonight. Let us head south. We'll take a boat to Sicily. My sister and her husband are there."

She put her hand on my chest and I felt her palm, soft as a cloud, warm as fresh-baked bread against my skin. It felt like home.

It would be a lie to say I didn't consider it. The four of us could be gone by tonight. Before the Vandals reach the southern roads. We could be halfway to Messina by the time anyone realized that we were missing, and anyone who knew I'd abandoned my post would be dead in a matter of days.

"No," I repeated.

Ceres cooed gently as she napped against her mother's breast. Lavinia moved her hand up to cup my face and tilted her head back to keep the tears that were welling in her eyes from falling.

The flower fell from her hair.

I went to check on Aelia later that night. I found her humming to herself in her room as she carved something into the wall with a bronze cooking knife. The song was familiar. It was something her mother used to sing when they were little, but I couldn't quite remember the words. I walked into the room and picked up the straw doll that sat on the edge of her bed. I'd brought it back for her at the end of my last campaign. Its head was made from the hollowed shell of an acorn and painted with white pigment while its body wore a dress fashioned from a leftover tuft of black wool harvested in Britania. I thought she would like it, but it looked as though it'd barely been touched.

Aelia looked over her shoulder and met my eyes, but then turned silently back to etching out her picture.

"A bit old to be playing with dolls, aren't you, Father?" she asked.

"True enough. Seems you've outgrown them as well. What are you carving?"

She leaned back and stretched out her legs, pointing with the blade. It showed a woman walking out of a cave surrounded by flowers that were blooming from barren land. It was skillfully done, despite the crude instrument used in its construction.

"It's Proserpina, returning from the underworld. I made it for Ceres. This will be her room soon enough."

"Another story you heard from Niall?"

"Yes. There certainly isn't anyone else here to tell me stories."

Now I saw the crux of the issue.

"You're mad because I've not been home."

"I don't care," she said quickly. "I'm nearly marrying age. I'll be out of the house just as soon as a worthy suiter makes his appearance, but Mother and Ceres have missed you."

"We've never lied to each other, Aelia. Let us not start now."

She glared at me from beneath the loose coils of black hair that fought their way free from her braid.

"I'll tell the truth if you will."

"It's a deal."

"Fine. Mother said that we would see you more now you've re-turned to Rome. She said leading the city guard meant you weren't going to be leaving anymore, but you're still never here. Why?"

I opened my mouth to speak but closed it again wordlessly. Aelia was just like her mother. She always seemed to cut right to the heart of things.

I'd just promised to speak the truth, yet how could I tell my daughter that this might be the last time she ever saw me? How could I explain to her that she would be going to Sicily and that I would remain to fight an impossible battle?

"All I've done has only ever been to protect you, your sister, your mother, and Rome."

"Protect us from what?"

"There are things outside these walls. Some of them are frightening things, monstrous things. I'd hoped you'd never learn of them, but some of them are on their way here."

"And you and the legion must fight them to protect the city?"

"I told you I would not lie. I'm going to do my best, but there's a strong chance that I won't be able to stop them this time."

Aelia's eyes softened and she nodded solemnly; her slender jaw set into a hard line that once again reminded me of her mother. She was no whiny merchant's daughter. She would not beg me to run or cry that her father was going to die. She was a child of the legion. She understood sacrifice.

"Will you stay until they arrive then?" she asked.

"I'll stay as long as I can."

I understood in the coming days why the *Graeca* of old saw the Sight as a curse.

I awoke from my wife's bed three mornings later to the sound of screams echoing throughout the city. I took my vigil at the northern peak of the Aurelian walls and looked out on the encroaching horde. Vandal colors coated the hills with their arrival. The sea of yellow wheat that once painted the horizon was trampled beneath waves of leather-clad boots.

I rallied what soldiers remained to the defenses. I'd had my men take every precaution. The *ballista* were armed and strung and every archer in the city was placed upon the ramparts, but there was little we could do. There was simply too much wall and not enough men to hold it. I watched helplessly as the brutes forced their way inside. Then the fighting spilled onto the streets.

I'm no stranger to the scent of blood, but never has it so fully permeated my senses. The sounds of screams and the red mist of slaughter filled every breath. Everywhere I looked, I saw the faces of the dead as their spirits rose from bloody corpses to begin the long march toward Plutonian shores.

"Centurian," one of the smaller ghosts called to me in the aftermath of the first day. I'd been limping in retreat toward the inner Servian wall, the last sanctum left in the city. "What happened to the square? Why has the emperor painted it red? Is there to be a triumph today?"

"No," I told him. "There is no triumph. You are dead."

"I don't understand. I can't be dead. My brother is expecting me in the morning. We were to go fishing in the sea. He was going to teach me how to work the nets."

I shook my head at the wraith and pointed in the direction the other spirits marched.

"Your brother will meet you in the Elysian Fields, specter. Follow the others. I'm sure you will find him."

The inner walls didn't hold any better than the outer ones. The *Magister Militum* and his officers were executed on the second day. I watched as the barbarians dragged them to the *Circus Maximus* from behind new walls that were not constructed by wood or stone, but by a sea of enemies that were impossible to pass. They brought the magister to the center of the theater and removed his fat head from his shoulders before a cheering crowd.

Then their leader, a heavily armored man named Geyseric, dragged our emperor to the streets like a stray dog to be rousted from the hearth. They tied him to the pole that carried the eagle standard, *his standard*, and made a mockery of him. They stripped him naked, cut his flesh, and pissed upon his feet.

I gathered what soldiers I could find and tried to scrap together a militia. *Praetors, vigils,* citizens, slaves—it didn't matter. I aimed to liberate our emperor and escort him to the lowlands where he still had armies that might safely escort him to Constantinople.

Our skirmishes were short and doomed to failure, however. Those who had been proud to call themselves Roman the day before were quick to love their new masters. They led the hordes to our secret sanctuaries in the catacombs and flushed us from them like rabbits chased by a hound. Yet as men fell around me, somehow, I continued to survive. Each day, I fought the Vandals and bathed in the blood of friends and enemies alike. Yet no arrows touched me. No blades kissed my skin.

"What do we do now?" asked one of the last soldiers under my command on the fifth day. We were hiding in the sewers like rats, watching as the Vandals dragged a line of Romans through the city in chains. There were only a handful of us now. The boy who asked couldn't have been more than fifteen summers. It was clear from the way he carried himself that his hands were more used to wielding a scythe than a spear, but he gripped the weapon tightly and kept his footing. That was more than most managed. It was probably why he was still alive.

"There's nothing to do but gather what resources the enemy hasn't already taken and flee," I told him. "Perhaps we can return with one of the *princeps'* armies and retake our home."

It was a lie. The stone would remain, but everything that gave the city life would be ashes by the time an army arrived. There would be no coming back.

Sweat beaded on the boy's brow, yet the relief in his eyes was plain.

I rushed home to gather what remained of my effects. I'd arranged passage for my family with a caravan of traveling merchants. Everything we owned that was of any value went with them, but there was a dagger that had belonged to my father. The iron was gray and pockmarked with age. It was an inferior blade that I would not trust in battle and would be worth little to sell, but I couldn't bear to leave it behind.

I thought it would be hard to give up the fight, but I'd be lying if I didn't admit that a small part of me felt relieved I was finally leaving. I didn't think I would survive the first day. I didn't dare to hope, even when I saw the second and the third. But now I could leave with my honor intact. I'd done my duty. My death couldn't save Rome now.

That feeling vanished when I saw my home.

I arrived to find the house in ruins. The men I'd paid to escort my family to safety weren't here, but Niall's body was abandoned on the step, his throat slit by a barbarian blade. The ground was spoilt with burnt cloth, shattered stoneware, and sticky blood. I saw the remains of my wedding bowl scattered across the courtyard and experienced a surge of fear, unlike anything I'd felt on a battlefield.

My heart beat with the speed of Mercury as I stepped across the threshold. The inside was empty of life save one man: a lone Vandal picking through my wife's possessions like a vulture. My precious Lavinia's body was on the floor. Her gaze was twisted in fear and hate, her hands still gripping the hilt of my father's blade. She'd driven it into her own chest. My children were nowhere to be seen.

The scavenger turned to face me as I entered the room where my family used to eat, laugh, and tell each other stories. He jabbered at me in their primitive, guttural tongue. Then he reached for a blade at his hip, but I was faster. I severed the hand at the wrist and pressed the tip of my sword against his throat. He screamed.

I considered what to do with him then. The thought of his bones breaking as I listened to the delicious choir of his wails gave rise to a primal pleasure that I felt churning in the base of my bowels. I could keep him alive for weeks if I wanted, bathing my wounded heart in his pain. I could cauterize his wrist, bind and gag him so his cries wouldn't attract the others, and then take my time with him. Diminishing him, piece by piece, until there was nothing left.

It was tempting, but there was no time. I killed him quickly.

I turned back to Lavinia as his corpse leaked its remaining blood upon my floor. She was dressed in her traveling clothes, her head and neck wrapped in linen that Aelia had woven for her from soft flax. It was stained now.

I dropped to my knees and ran my hand along her cheek. The skin was cold.

I felt something inside me fracture. I loved Lavinia as much as any man could. We used to sneak into the fisherman's carts when were children. We'd ride them to Focene to swim in the ocean and spend the afternoon reciting fables as we dried our naked bodies on the sand. Then her father died and her mother married a man who beat her. Lavinia would show up with bruises some days, but I lived in fear that one day she wouldn't show up at all.

I started entering sword competitions to win money so that I could marry her. I was a boy of only thirteen, but I was fast. I defeated men twice my size using my father's rust-pocked dagger. I even managed to impress Titus enough that he let an orphaned brat with no status join the legion two years early. He gave me a real sword. He even gave me the money I needed to marry Lavinia out of his own wages back when he was just the local *centenarius*. When I asked him how I could repay this debt, he merely told me to 'use that sword for the betterment of Rome.'

Since then, I have dedicated my entire life to the preservation, study, and improvement of the Roman Empire. Now it was gone, and so was she.

I couldn't bear to look at her like this. I don't pretend to understand the minds of these brutes, nor do I wish to, but I know that such rampant hate can't stem from simple ignorance. Perhaps it was the machinations of their savage gods that bid them to defile so recklessly.

And where were our gods? Why did they not protect us?

I supposed it didn't matter now.

"Lavinia," I said. "Why are you in our house? You should have been to Sicily already. You weren't supposed to be here."

Her eyes were still. They glistened like philosopher's glass. I fished some coins from my purse and placed one on each of them for Charon's fee. Then I removed my father's dagger from her chest and made a pyre of our home.

"I'm so sorry. I've failed in my promise. I should have protected you."

Flames quickly licked their way up the walls, burning the house where Lavinia birthed our children. Once the blaze had taken hold, I mounted the looter's horse and rode for the gates as fast as I could, taking the messenger's pass. My only fortune, if it can be called such, was that the road was poorly guarded. Too many men were busy picking at the bones of the eternal empire. I only managed to kill two more before I exited the city. Would that it were a dozen—that it were all of them.

The knowledge that my children were not there was a mercy, though a small one. The Vandals were not gentle with those they took as slaves. Still, it was a chance.

I rode for two days and nights, giving the horse no mercy. I cut through the forest to the east, past their patrols, and continued up the trails along the mountainside. This particular horde was gathered from the tribes to the north. I'd fought the Vandals many times, but my campaigns never took me to their cold and rotten homeland. They would be traveling along Roman roads, but wouldn't think to check the mountain paths. They were used by foragers and shepherds. They were narrow and precarious. Even a lone traveler like me could meet his end by plummeting down the dire slopes if he wasn't careful. There was no room for marching armies.

Even so, I took the trails with reckless speed. I needed to get ahead of the Vandals. That way, I could track their movement from the hills without ever encountering the dominant force in the light of day. Then, when Apollo's chariot carried the sun behind the sea, I would sneak down to their camps and search for my children.

It was a foolish plan, I knew, but it was the only one I had. Aelia and Ceres could be in any one of a hundred convoys... if they were even still alive.

More than once, I wondered if I should have simply stayed in Rome and resolved myself to kill as many as I could before I fell. Then I would have been able to meet Pluto with pride, as a centurion should. But every time I thought about turning back, I saw the image of Lavinia's face and pressed my heels into the horse's sides. I dared not picture Aelia or Ceres, lest my mind play tricks and show me false visions of their fate.

I gave in to my mount's pants and whines on the third day. We stopped in the cradle of a valley where a small stream slid through the curvature of the ground. It was a bright and beautiful place, full of colour and life.

I sat on the grass. It had a spongy texture that had absorbed much of the sun's warmth. I listened to the trickling of the stream and the rustling of the wind in the trees for a while, watching the horse have its drink. I should have felt a semblance of peace, basking in the serenity of the valley. Nature's beauty should have served as a balm for my wounded soul. It did not. Without the treacherous trail or the pain of the saddle to focus on, my mind was free to reflect and drown in the depths of my regret. I wondered what I had done to the gods for them to taunt me with such beauty when my heart was weighed down with so much darkness.

Then the exhaustion of the week seemed to compound and come crashing down on me all at once. I lay back and cried as I had not since childhood, shielding my face from Apollo's sight.

I must have fallen asleep at some point. It seemed only a moment passed before I opened my eyes, but the sun had long since begun its descent behind the mountain. I looked around the gap and realized that my steed was nowhere to be seen.

"Horse!" I cried, sending echoes across the valley. The creature gave no response.

I quickly drank my fill from the stream and started following the beast's trail as best I could. I have little skill as a tracker, but the animal's hooves left such deep prints in the loamy earth that even a novice like me could follow them. It seemed he grazed the area for some time before venturing onto a nearby trail that headed further up the mountain.

The terrain was steep. The fertile ground of the valley turned hard and grew ever rockier as I climbed, making the horse's tracks increasingly difficult to follow. It was unusual for a beast to choose such an awkward climb unbidden. This trail held no promise of water or sustenance, both of which were in the valley below. So why would it come this way?

I couldn't leave without it, though. Having little food and even less coin, a strong horse was far too valuable a thing to leave behind. Besides, we might need it if we're to make a quick escape.

After just over an hour of searching, I finally found the creature. Its reins were ensnared in a tangled patch of thorny vines. It cried and tugged at the leather straps, only serving to cut its maw and ensnare itself further.

"Foolish beast," I said, pulling my father's knife from its sheath. "This fate serves you."

It took nearly all the day's remaining light to calm the creature enough that I could cut it free. Even upon its release, it seemed wild. Its eyes were crazed and its mouth was nearly frothing.

"What is it? Do you smell something?"

The horse continued to tug in the direction it had been heading before it got itself snagged. It pulled and whined. The pale creature's eyes nearly bulged out of its skull.

Logic told me to keep the animal's head down and lead it back to the bottom of the mountain. That was the direction the Vandals would be taking their slaves and carrying their ill-gotten wealth. Curiosity defeated me in the end, however. I straddled the horse and slowly allowed it to take me onward.

It took a great deal of effort to keep us moving at a safe pace. Without guidance or incentive, the horse trekked further and further up the mountain. We occasionally crossed ledges and thick walls of bramble that appeared to go nowhere, only to find ourselves emerging on yet another trail.

I eventually started to notice other markings on the path. I'd marched in enough campaigns to recognize the signs of a *contubernium* passing through. The scuffed ground, refuse, and scraps of food here didn't come from an army, but from a small band. Perhaps a dozen or so legionnaires.

But the ones who marked this trail might not have been part of the legion at all. Maybe a band of scouts from the horde were exploring the mountain in search of food or checking for signs of an ambush. Either case would be fine with me, but I hoped it was Vandals. I was eager to send more of them to meet their dark gods.

It was clear the horse knew where it was going. Either it had been here before or some form of intrinsic beast sense was leading it. My instructor told me of such things when I first learned how to ride.

"*If you're ever lost, your horse will lead you back to safety,*" he said. "*If ever you have a thirst, your horse will lead you to drink. And if ever there is a danger, your horse will know about it long before you do.*"

We were crossing a particularly steep ledge when I began to hear a strange sound on the wind. It was barely noticeable at first, a tickle of pleasant melody that vibrated amidst the whisper of the breeze. But then I realized that it was a woman's voice that made the air tremble.

She was singing a song unlike anything I'd heard before. It went into my ears like the fingers of Venus, plucking gently on the strings of my broken heart. Faint as the sound was, I understood my mount's desire to charge head-first into the coming night.

We continued onward with the voice as our beacon. I gave less consideration to hampering my steed's movements as we grew closer and started urging it through the darkness. We leaped thickets of thorn, climbed loose stones, and nearly fell to our deaths more than once. Still, we pressed on. It was only when the last rays of light were disappearing into the velvet sky that we arrived at the source.

Pushing our way through the dense bush, we came upon a cave set into the mountainside. The entrance was twice as tall as a man and rimmed with jagged teeth. It looked like a great yawning mouth, ready to swallow any who would enter deep into the Earth.

Those whose markings I'd seen on the trail were here as well. There were five Vandals outside the cave's maw. Three of them were struggling to tie up a row of slaves, eyes darting between the rope in their fumbling fingers and the source of the music. The other two were guarding the cave's mouth, though holding their post seemed to be taking all of their resolve. It was clear the voice called to them, just as it called to me.

Then I noticed something else that set my heart to pound with more force than the hammers of Vulcan's forge. There was a little girl with them. Her hair was matted with filth and a bruise had swollen one side of her face, turning it a nasty shade of purple, but I knew her. It was Niall's daughter, Mila. I was sure of it. And she carried in her arms a small bundle that looked to be the size of a child. I said a silent prayer of thanks to the huntress Diana for using my horse to guide me here.

I got down from the creature's back. A mounted charge would have been better if we were out in the open, but there was no space to maneuver and the footing was too uneven.

"Thank you for bringing me here," I whispered to the animal, after quietly leading him out of the Vandal's earshot. "You've done very well. May you lead a long and healthy life."

Then I slapped his flanks and watched my last friend ride off into the distance.

The song was heavy at the mountain's peak. It was beyond alluring. The sound made it hard to think of anything except walking into that cave. I could feel its melody resonating throughout my entire body, humming at my fingertips.

I tried to shut it out. This task demanded focus. Fortunately, the barbarians were distracted by the song as well. That was to my advantage.

I crept through the brush to the edge of their camp and slowly drew my sword from its sheath. The familiar ring of steel cut through the air, but no one heard it. The sound was lost in the thrum of the woman's song.

Of the three Vandals managing the slaves, one had finished his knots and was busy hammering stakes into the ground. The other two were still struggling to secure their prisoners.

I moved swiftly toward the one driving in the stakes. He didn't hear me coming. The music was too loud. I drove my blade through his throat mid-hammer-stroke and then slashed a second barbarian across the torso before he had time to scream.

Then I killed the third as he struggled to untangle his hands from the bindings to draw his sword. He looked young, I noticed that his upper lip was only just getting its first wisps of hair before I saw the light go out of his eyes. The two who had been standing guard were faster. They had their blades out and were ready to fight.

I'm an excellent swordsman, but fighting two warriors at once without a shield to guard your flank is difficult at the best of times. These savages weren't novices either. They moved together, taking turns creating openings in my defense for the other to exploit. I felt the fiery bite of steel along the edge of my ribs as one of them slipped their blade between the panels of my lorica. I cried out in pain. It wasn't a fatal wound, but it might as well have been. I could no longer raise my sword over my head.

I retreated, using the thick brush to hamper their movements. It slowed them down, but I was only buying time. Soon I found myself with my back against the precipice of the mountain. There was nowhere left to run. One of the Vandals muttered something to his friend in their crude tongue, inciting a malevolent laugh.

They started to advance, pushing me to the edge, and I knew this would be my end.

Then the laughing man tripped. He fell face-first into the craggy stone, leaving his companion to face me alone. Without taking the time to marvel at my impossible luck, I seized my chance and lunged at the other. We exchanged three blows before I managed to slide under his guard. My blade found its way into an undefended lung. Blood burbled to the man's lips as he slid off my sword and began the long tumble down the cliff face.

The second man was still struggling to get to his feet. Now that the other was dead, I realized he hadn't tripped from his own clumsiness but rather *was tripped.* I saw my Mila clinging to his leg as the man kicked at her shoulders, trying to knock her loose.

I took my sword and drove it through his mouth until the tip dripped crimson from the back of his skull.

"Mila," I said, rushing forward and sweeping the child into a tight hug. "Where's Aeilia and Ceres?"

"Ceres is fine," she said, wiping a tear from the eye that hadn't swollen shut. "One of the other women is holding her by the cave. Aelia is inside. One of those men took her in there. I don't know why. I didn't understand what they were saying. But Dominus, your wife... She tried to fight them, but there were so many. She told us to run, but I fear..."

"I found her body in the house beside your father's," I said, drawing my dagger and using it to cut the bonds that were still wrapped around her wrists. "I've paid their toll and their souls have been laid to rest. Though I fear the ruin of my house is an image I will carry with me until we meet them in Elysium."

"I'm sorry, Dominus."

"Why were you still in Rome? Why did you not leave with the merchants I paid? You were supposed to be leagues away when the attack started."

"Rumors of the Vandals spread among the merchants. Some of them got nervous about leaving Rome's walls. They got into an argument and delayed their departure. Then the guards they hired turned on them when the attack started. They killed the merchants, stole their goods, and fled. Papa was trying to secure a new route for us in your stead, but all the *mercēnārius* had been bought up. Domina was going to have us leave your wealth behind and take our chances on the road, but the Vandals arrived too soon."

The rope finally snapped and slithered from her wrists like a dead serpent falling to the ground.

"Don't go in the cave," she said, grabbing my wrist.

"You just said that Aelia is in there."

"I know. It's just... That singing... It's wrong."

I looked at her and saw the fear her swollen face couldn't conceal. Her good eye was wide with panic, just as the horse's had been when it was trapped in its nest of thorns.

The song didn't seem evil. On the contrary, it promised a salve for the anguish that burdened my soul. I remembered Niall's story about the siren who bewitched Remus and Romulus. Could it be true? I've seen many strange magicks and dark horrors in my time. I've seen priests use their smokes and herbs to summon visions from the gods. I've seen scorpions with the faces of men and fish-tailed women basking on rocky shores. Somehow, this seemed different.

There was no point in wondering, though. Aelia was inside. That was all that mattered.

"Give me your sleeve," I told her.

She held out he arm obediently. I ripped a length from the linen sleeve and rolled up the cloth. Then I packed it under my lorica so that it pressed against the cut in my side, slowing the flow of blood. It wasn't perfect, but it would have to do. Then I took one of the dead men's blades and handed it to Mila.

"Cut the others loose and protect Ceres, I will return."

I took a moment to find a dry enough branch from which I could make a torch with oil and flint. There was no more room for hesitation. My heart released the fear it had clenched since I first saw my wife's cold hands clenching that blade.

The singing was louder inside the cave. It seemed to resonate in the very stone of the mountain. I realized with a measure of guilt that finding my daughter wasn't my only reason for exploring this darkness. The song was in no language I knew, and yet I understood it perfectly. It promised to erase my past and all memory of what I've lost. Such beautiful gifts as the gods themselves could scarcely grant. I needed to see what manner of creature could produce such an ethereal cadence.

The air in here felt warm, though it appeared damp and tasted of mold and earth. The footing was uneven. It sloped steadily downward, giving the sickening feeling of falling with every step.

Finally, I came to the source of the sound. The tunnel opened up to a wide cavern adorned with crystalline walls that glimmered and amplified my torchlight in waves of green and blue. It was large enough to rival the coliseum itself. The entire mountain must have been hollow to accommodate such a grand enclosure. An underground lake was at its center. The water was deep, black, and still as death.

The barbarian held Aelia at the edge of the water. He didn't seem to notice me, even as my torchlight harmonized with his in the crystal walls. His focus was entirely on the water. Good. Killing him would be that much easier.

I walked over to him, quiet as death, and raised my sword to strike, but then something odd happened. My arm was suddenly paralyzed. I tried to will myself to bring down my blade and smite this last enemy, but it was as if the limb no longer belonged to me. It was as immovable as the very mountain in which we stood. I'd killed hundreds of men across half a dozen battlefields. Never before has my sword arm failed to strike. Then the song grew even louder and all thought of killing the monster before me vanished. My entire body seemed to freeze in place.

The experience wasn't uncomfortable. It was the opposite. I was adrift on a tide of gentle solace. Warmth spread from my chest, all the way to my toes and fingertips, quelling the ache of the cut on my side and washing away the burden of my sins and failures. I felt weightless. All the animosity in me simply trickled away as I basked in the light of the song. It was akin to that feeling of being unable to get out of bed when nestled beneath woolen blankets on a chilly morning.

The Vandal turned and smiled at me. He was missing an eye. The cut had scabbed over, but the wound was fairly new. He must have gotten it in the battle. His sword rested at his side. He seemed equally uninterested in battle.

"Father?" Aelia asked. "What are you doing here?"

"I came to get you," I told her.

"You should leave. Before it's too late."

"Why would I leave?"

Aelia looked like she was struggling to explain, but something was keeping her from conjuring the words. Then the singing stopped.

The air grew cold in an instant. The fear that had been subdued by the woman's voice finally grew loud enough for me to hear it screaming. The Vandal didn't matter, I realized. The song was far more dangerous.

A ripple formed in the center of the lake, and from its trembling surface came a beautiful girl, naked but for the glistening water clinging to her skin. It enveloped her flesh like a gown, texturing her with an ephemeral sheen of fluid. Her hair flowed in twists and bends, exuding a ghastly pale radiance. Closer and closer she came until she reached the water's edge. Pale, sightless eyes looked through me with Plutonian beauty. She extended a slender palm.

I did not accept it.

"Come," she said in the lyrical voice that had driven me so close to madness. "Take my hand."

Without intention, my arm rose to meet her of its own accord.

"Don't do it," Aelia said.

I needed to run. I needed to grab my daughter, sprint out of this cave and not stop until we reached the sea. My mind was screaming to flee, though my body still would not obey.

The sensation was no longer comfortable. Rather than a warm bed, it now reminded me of those cold nights on the peninsula that I spent pinned to the ground under a mountain of corpses. I could almost hear the sound of human laughter that came from the dog-like Crocotta as they gnawed the bones of soldiers who died under my command. Struggling seemed useless; escape, hopeless. In a final effort, I focused all my energy, all of my strength on stopping my arm.

It hesitated.

The girl looked down. The smallest of smiles crossed her pale lips.

Like a whisper from the divine, she sang, cruel and desperate. It was a hopeless song of loss, intimately uttered. Her empty eyes saw into my very essence and conjured me to her command. There was nothing I could do.

"Your heart is full of pain," she said, delicately tracing the lines that ran through my palm with a soft finger. "You seek an end. You seek death."

"No."

"You cannot lie to me, centurion. I see it in your heart. It aches for your wife. These savages took her from you," she gestured with her hand toward the frozen Vandal. It seemed the song's enchantment had worn off on him as well. His mouth was contorted into a silent scream of agony as his remaining eye darted between us. "They're crude tools. But I'm grateful they stumbled upon my mountain. I've waited centuries for my revenge. Now it's finally complete."

She hummed a lilting tune, and the Vandal seemed to regain control of his face.

"What reward would you like for your service?" she asked him.

He shouted something. I may not understand their tongue, but I know its intent couldn't have been pleasant. Then he spat on her.

The woman frowned at that.

She took the sword from my hand and ran the man through with it. He cried out in agony, but never moved. It wasn't until the last of his blood ran along the edge of my blade and streamed into the pool that his body finally collapsed, plunging into the icy water. Some of it splashed onto the woman. Inky tendrils of crimson stretched their way across her liquid gown.

"I detest rudeness," she said.

My reflexes strained against my frozen muscles as I tried to get between her and Aelia, but they wouldn't budge. I might as well have tried to lift the pantheon.

She watched me struggling and flashed her opalescent teeth. Then she sang another verse.

I tried to deny her again, but I couldn't muster the strength. Every inch of me ached to accept the gift of oblivion her song promised.

"Would you like to see your wife again?" she asked. My sword still dripped with the blood of the Vandal in her hand.

My heart screamed to accept. The paralysis no longer mattered. I would have opened my arms to her if she let me.

"I'm sorry, Aelia," I said.

I'm sorry, Lavenia.

"Do not apologize Hadrian. Fight," said another voice. I couldn't tell where it came from at first, but it was a voice that I knew. It was the voice that sang to our children. The voice that helped me to sleep when the wraiths of past battlefields returned to haunt my midnight hours. And with that voice came a scent I recognized as. The stench of the damp cave was overwhelmed with the delicate scent of violet *paeonias.*

Then a specter appeared beside me. This ghost did not look like the ones I saw lingering in the wreckage of Rome, though. Could I trust my eyes? It was as if my wife was standing beside me again. She appeared solid, as real as she had been when I came home from my first campaign and found her with our daughter at her breast. I saw warmth and life in her. It broke my heart to know it was a lie.

"I can't do this alone," I told her, my voice cracking.

"You must," she said. "Aelia lives. Ceres lives. You have a duty."

"I've not the strength."

"Then find it," she said, snapping her gaze back to me. "You will not abandon our daughters. You will find the strength to leave this cave, Hadrian. I will not permit you to die."

Then the woman in the lake sang a sharp note, and suddenly Lavinia was gone again. She snarled as her grip tightened on my wrist.

"No more ghosts," she said. She thrust the blade toward my heart, and with a rush of will, I managed to pivot. It wasn't much. A simple half step accompanied by a rolling of the shoulder, but it was just enough that the sword glanced off my pauldron instead of killing me.

She slashed the blade where my belly would have been, only I once again managed to step back. Not completely out of reach, but just enough that the blade's tip only managed to scratch the leather surface of my lorica.

"You're a strange one," she said, cocking her head like a bird as she lowered the weapon. "That much is certain."

She looked more curious than angry now. She stepped in close, sniffing at my neck. I felt helpless as a rabbit in the jaws of a fox. Then she stepped back, her nose crinkled into a foul expression that blemished her otherwise beautiful face.

"Blood of Ares," she spat. I recognized the name. It was what the old *Graeca* called Mars, the God of War. "I can smell him on you. It's diluted, but it's there, like a filthy disease. There was a time when I would have killed you both just for being that monster's brood, but not today, I think. I've no interest in you, anyway."

She turned to Aelia.

"I'm more interested in you, girl," she said, stepping toward her. She moved like a dancer, but there was something cat-like in her step, too. Something predatory. "Did you know I destroyed your home? I sent the men who sacked your city and killed your mother. Would you like revenge?"

My daughter glared at her with a look I'd seen many times before. There was iron in her eyes.

Aelia had always been disobedient. I'd caught her sneaking out to watch plays in the city square more than once, but it went back even further than that. I remembered the day I first saw her. I'd been away at war when she was born, but I'll never forget when I returned home. It had been a twenty-day march, but Lavinia wouldn't even let me sit down before she put my daughter in my arms for the first time. Aelia was not a quiet child. She kicked and screamed so loudly that I felt as if I'd drank one of the priest's vitality tinctures. The sound of her newly formed lungs sapped away the fatigue and snapped my senses back to full alertness. Everyone in the *rione* must have heard her. She was born defiant.

"I want nothing from you," she said.

The woman in the water laughed. "Not just Ares' blood, but his spirit as well, I see. Won't you even hear what I have to offer?"

"It does not matter the type of poisoned fruit you give me. I will not eat it."

The woman laughed a second time. The sound was much less pleasant than her singing.

"Listen anyway, child. I may yet perk your appetite. I've been alive for a long time and I've been trapped in this cave for the better part of it. Romulus' *mágos* were thorough in building their prison. The only way for me to leave this place is in death."

"Then you want us to kill you?" Aelia asked.

"Gladly," I said. "Release me and I'll give you the end you seek."

"Oh yes. You've mete out death to many, haven't you, centurion? I can smell that on you, too. You reek of corpses. That woman wasn't the first soul to pass through your bloody hands, was she? Go on then. Try it."

Suddenly, I felt control come back to my limbs. I almost fell over from the shock of it. The woman extended my sword out to me.

In a flash of crimson mist, I took the blade from her and drove it deep into her heart. She didn't even have time to step away. Her body crumpled and fell into my arms, her naked legs splashing. Her blood ran down my arm and streamed into the water, mixing with its tortured waves.

She appeared more human up close. Her hair was a dark and mottled brown. Her skin was soft and young, without scars or cracks. What I held in my arms seemed nothing more than a girl, perhaps one that my daughters might resemble in a few years. But then she looked up at me and smiled.

"Not enough," she said.

She pushed herself away from me and pulled the blade from her chest. I watched as the threads of her heart stitched themselves back together and the skin between her breasts closed until there wasn't even so much as a blemish to mark the fatal wound.

"What are you?" I asked.

"Old, sated, and eager to rest." She turned back to Aelia. "But the power in my blood won't let me die. The only way to leave this cave is to pass my power to another woman. One who is strong, and would use that power to seek vengeance on the men who've hurt them. I've instructed these men to bring you here because I've heard your song. It seeks power." Her eyes glimmered. "What say you, child? I used my voice to break the empire of the wolf—the greatest civilization the world has ever known. Imagine what you could do against a scattered horde of barbarians."

I stepped between Aelia and the woman.

"You stay away from her."

She scowled. I was certain she was going to use that voice to end me, but then I felt Aelia's slender hand on my sword arm as she stepped around my back. Now her steely gaze was fixed on me.

"I accept," she said.

"Aelia no. Leave this cave. I will hold her here. Take your sister and escape before it's too late."

"I'm sorry Father, but no," she shook her head, and I saw a sorrow as deep and excruciating as the one that dwelled in me behind the iron in her eyes.

"I watched Mother die," she said, her voice quiet as a prayer. "The others ran when the Vandals attacked, but I couldn't leave her. I gave Ceres to Mila and went back. She tried to fight them—cut that one across the eye," she nudged the scarred one with her toe. "But there were too many of them. Then she saw me. Her eyes found mine, and she knew. She knew I wouldn't leave her, so she turned her knife to her own breast and..."

"Aelia–"

"I've never felt so helpless in my life," she continued. "I wanted to save her, but there was nothing I could do. Even you, father. You're so strong, but even you couldn't save us. I won't be helpless anymore. I have to protect Ceres. You aren't strong enough. I will take this power and use it to call to the wolf that lives in every Roman. We shall prowl the entire world, hunting these creatures from our empire like the beasts they are."

My daughter stood tall, and I realized that she had grown while I was at war. Her body was no longer the small fragile thing that used to chase butterflies and hunt frogs by the Tiber. Her limbs were long and lank. She was older now than I was when I first took up the sword to earn her mother's hand.

The woman in the water smiled. She held out her arms again, but this time there was an edge of fear in her eyes. I supposed that no matter how old she was or how willing to meet Pluto in his ethereal halls, there was a part of her that was still human, and every human is at least a little afraid of death.

"Strike quickly," she said, her voice quivering. "Strike true."

Aelia took my father's knife from my belt. It was an old, gray, and ugly thing. But it seemed to shine in her hands. She stepped into the water and screamed as she drove the blade into the woman's heart.

The witch's arms wrapped around her, sealing the blow in a tight embrace. Then she whispered something into my daughter's ear and her body finally went limp.

The water that had clung to her like a bridal gown cascaded back to the lake and her body suddenly seemed ordinary. Just a dead girl with iron in her heart.

I walked over to Aelia and pulled the woman's body off her. She was shaken but otherwise seemed unharmed. She stopped me when I moved to throw the corpse into the lake.

"No. She's spent too long in this dark place to be able to rest here. Let's take her outside, underneath the stars."

So, I carried the nameless woman outside and built a pyre on the mountaintop. Mila and the other captives helped. Many of them were bruised and battered. All of them shared the same haunted expression. It was a look shared by all of those who had seen the end of civilization.

"What happened to the song?" one of them asked.

"There is no more song," I told him. Though I wasn't sure if it was true.

They gathered stones for the base and dry wood for the flame. I sprinkled the last of the oil from my pouch on her and struck a spark to ignite our tribute to this ancient horror.

"It's more than she deserves," I said to Aelia as we watched the woman's skin crack and her muscles be reduced to cinders.

"No one gets what they deserve, Father."

The light danced in her eyes as she held her sister and watched the fire.

"This changes our plans," she said after a long pause.

"This changes nothing. We go south, to Sicily. Your aunt is there. You and Ceres will be safe."

"No father. We go east to Constantinople," she said. There was an authority in her voice now. "It might take years or even decades for me to master this power, but I will need a vast city of men from which to build a suitable army. I shall forge Constantinople into the seat of a new empire, and I will use it to purge these monsters from our land."

The pyre burned all through the night, keeping us warm and leaving nothing of the woman save a few shards of bone and ash. We started the long descent down the mountain in the morning. Ceres had cried for her mother in the night, but now she slept like the dead against my chest. I would have been worried for her safety were it not for the tickle of warm breath on my shoulder. I still couldn't believe my luck in finding them, in surviving all of this madness. The gods must still be watching over us, after all.

And as we walked, Aelia started to hum. It was the same song she'd been humming when I found her carving the mural in her room. It was the one she learned from her mother—the one I could never quite remember the words to—and I realized as the melody flowed from her lungs that I would never deny her. Aelia and Ceres were my world now. I failed to protect Lavinia. I failed to protect Rome. But this time was different. I would not fail again.

Acknowledgements

This collection was written over the course of ten years. There are so many people to thank that it is, unfortunately, impossible to count them all. It took dozens, if not hundreds, of teachers, friends, family members, and encouraging strangers. Yet I will endeavor to thank those who deserve it most.

The first person I have to thank is my wife, Shelby. She is my first reader when I complete a draft, my first editor when I seek to improve it, and my most helpful critic when it is done. She's also the love of my life in her off hours. It's only thanks to her encouragement and patience that I could pursue this dream. Thanks for not strangling me when I ask you to pause the TV and be a sounding board so I can talk my way through plot holes, love. It means everything.

The other boundless source of encouragement in my life has been my mother. Sometimes I worry that I've not done enough to earn her seemingly unshakable faith in me, but I swear that I'll never fail to be grateful for it. She encouraged my love of reading from a young age, and despite being a single mother of four living on a tight budget, she always set money aside to buy me books when I asked for them.

There's my grandpa, Stephan, who read to me when I was small and always insisted that I have a fundamental knowledge of historical myths and legends. There are my brothers, Dakota, Branden, and Jeremy, who never fail to hold me up when I'm feeling low.

Lastly, I'd like to thank the teachers and librarians that I have had the privilege of learning from. This book wouldn't exist without you.

-Cody

About the Author

Cody D. Campbell is an author of science fiction and fantasy. He teaches creative writing at Linn Benton Community College and is the founder of Wraithwood Press. His work has been published by the *North Dakota Quarterly, Tales,* and *Writer's Digest.*

California-born, he currently lives in Oregon with his wife Shelby and their plucky Jack Russell mix, Echo, where he is currently working on publishing his debut novel, *Geppetto's Children.*

Website: codydcampbell.com

Instagram: instagram.com/cody_campbell_writer/

Facebook: facebook.com/gaming/codydcampbellwriter

TikTok: tiktok.com/@codydcampbell

To inquire about booking Cody D. Campbell for a speaking engagement, please contact Wraithwood Press at wraithwoodpress@gmail.com.